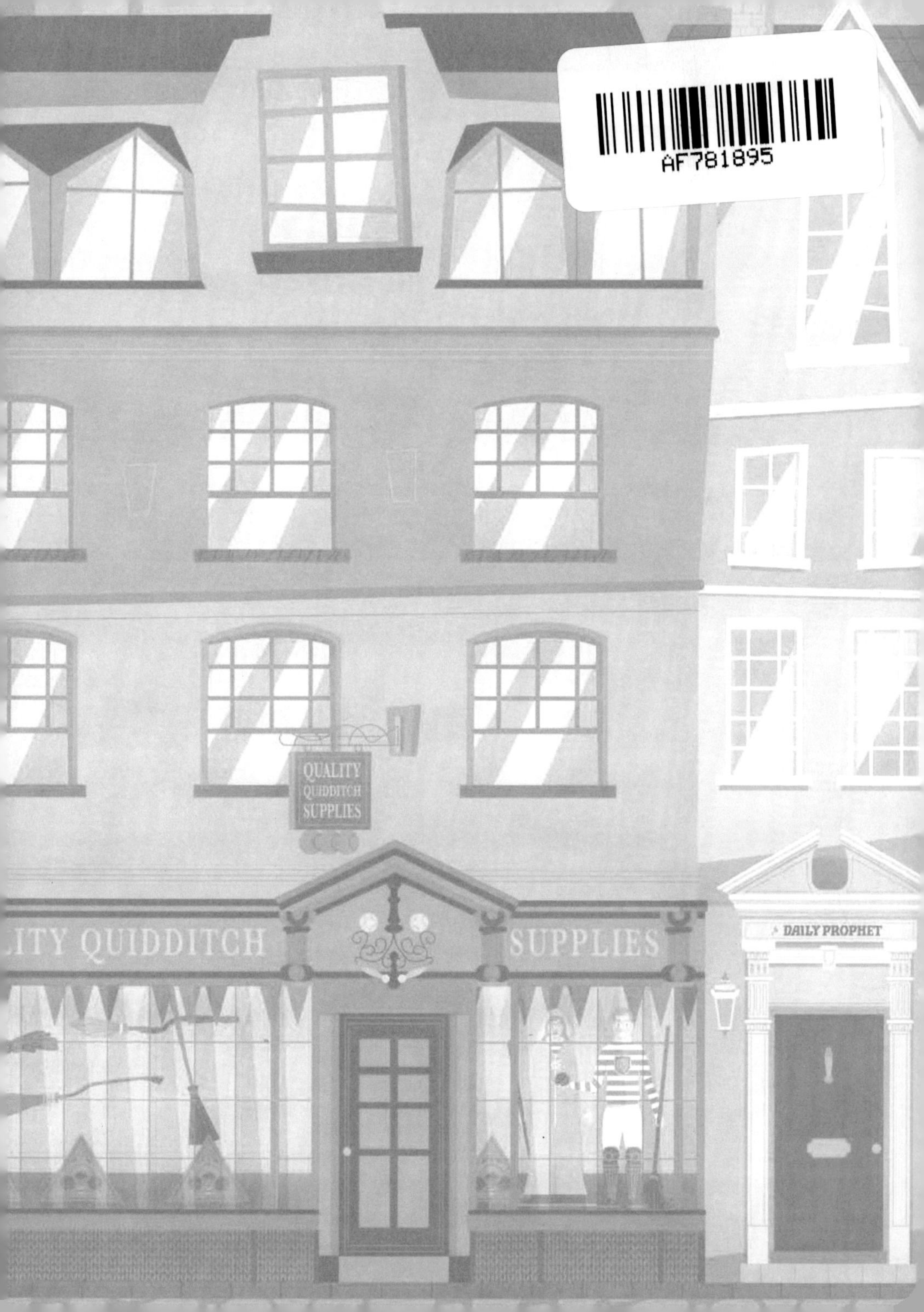
QUALITY
QUIDDITCH
SUPPLIES
LITY QUIDDITCH
SUPPLIES
DAILY PROPHET

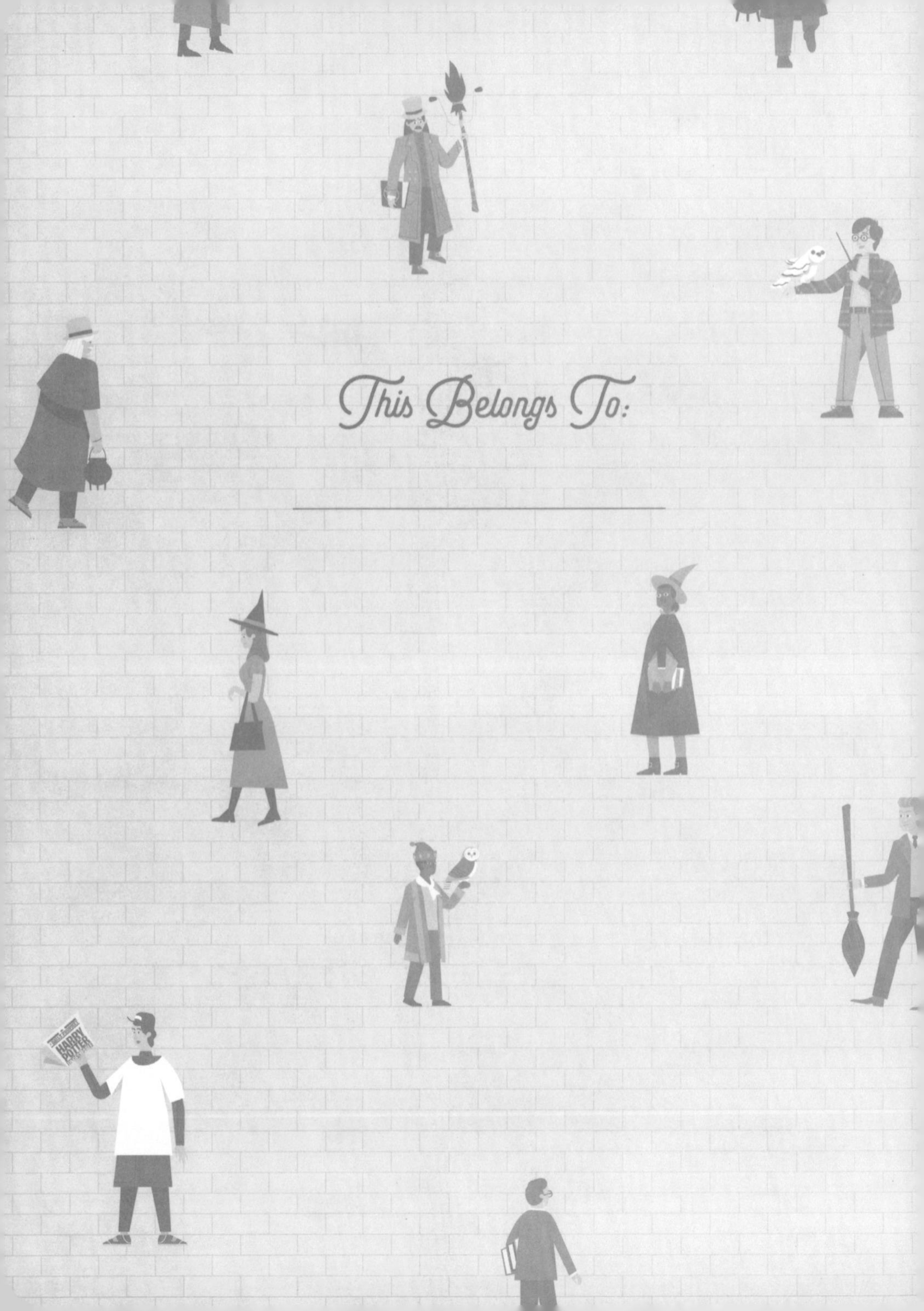

This Belongs To:

____

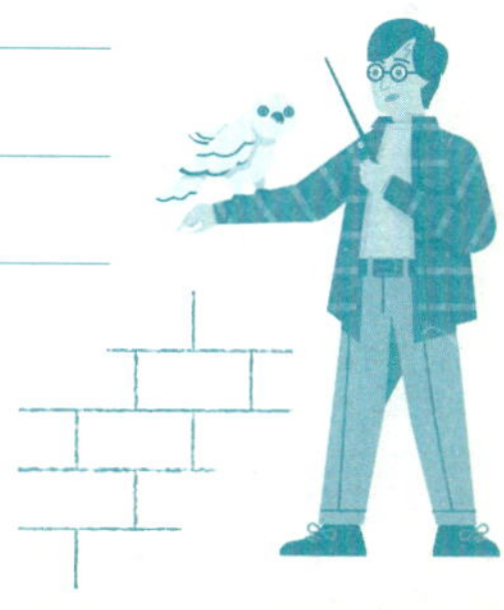

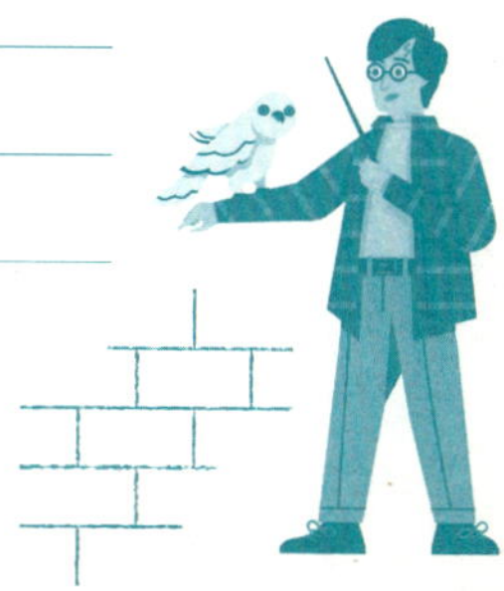

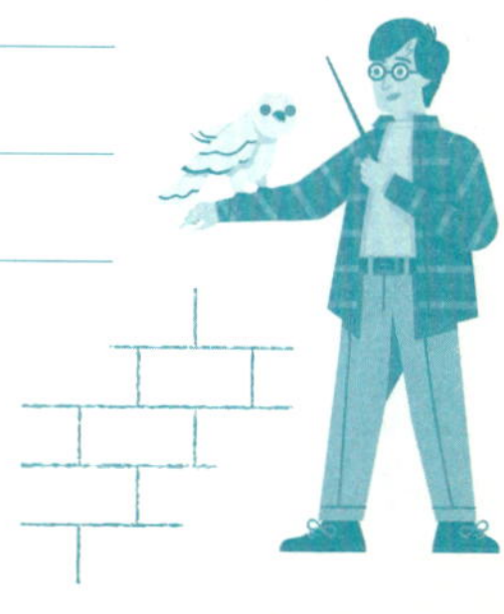

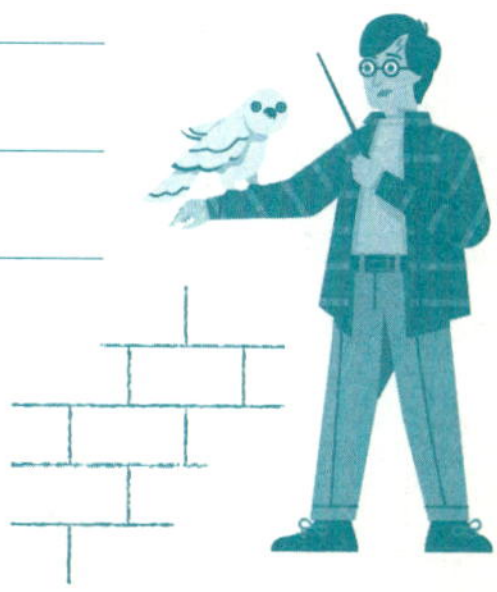

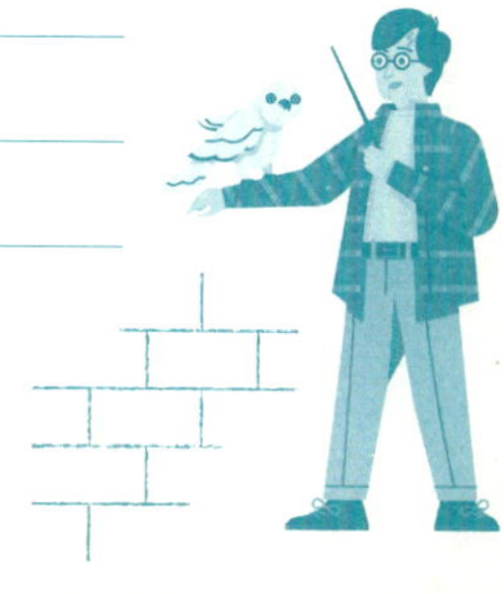

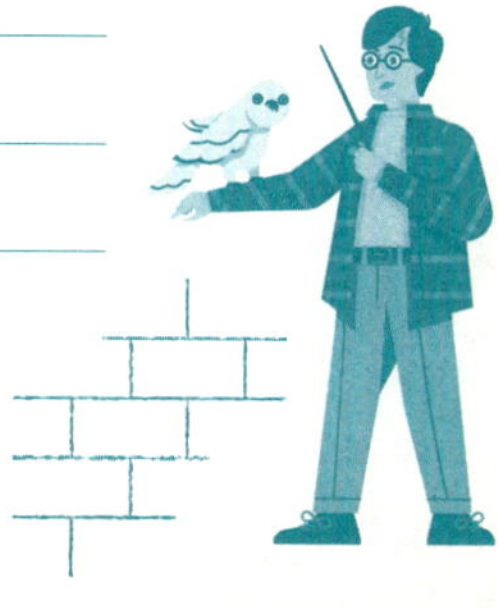

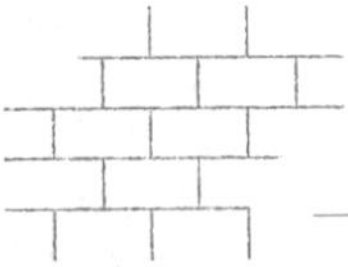

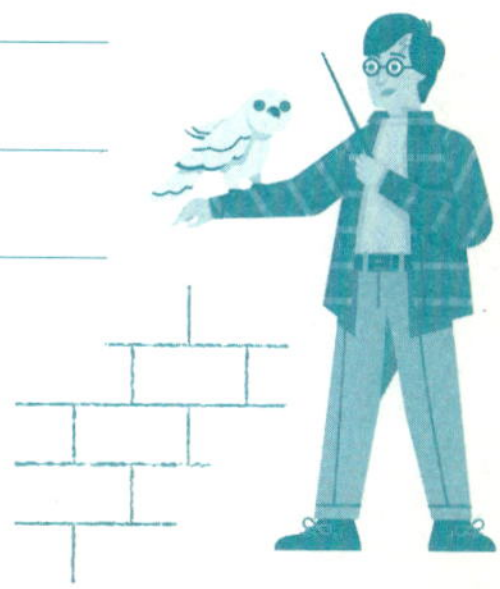

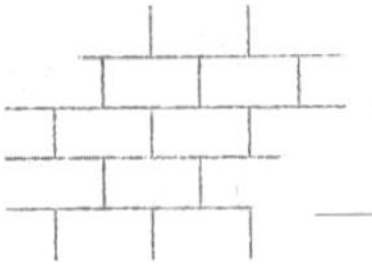

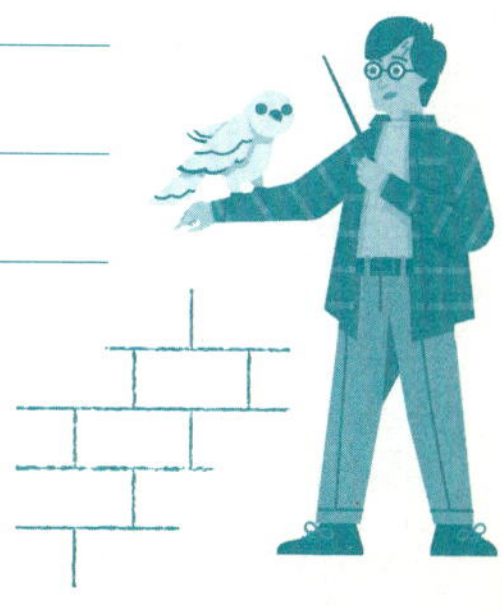

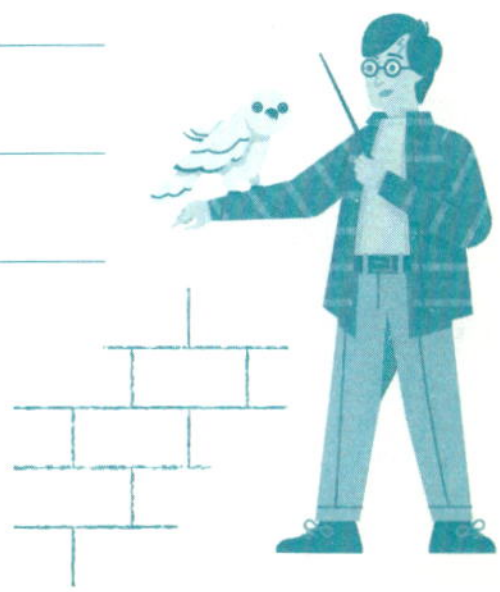

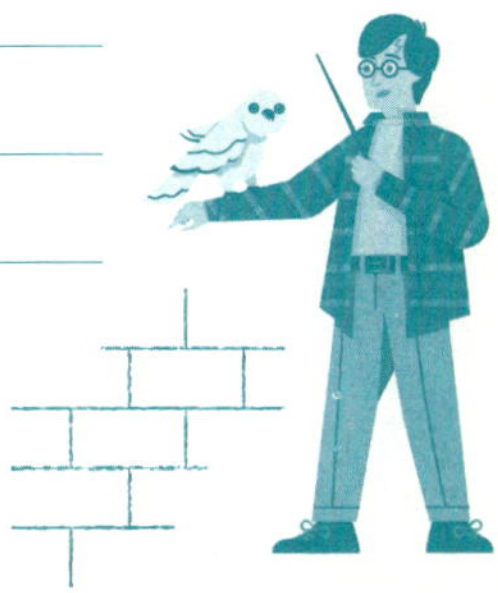

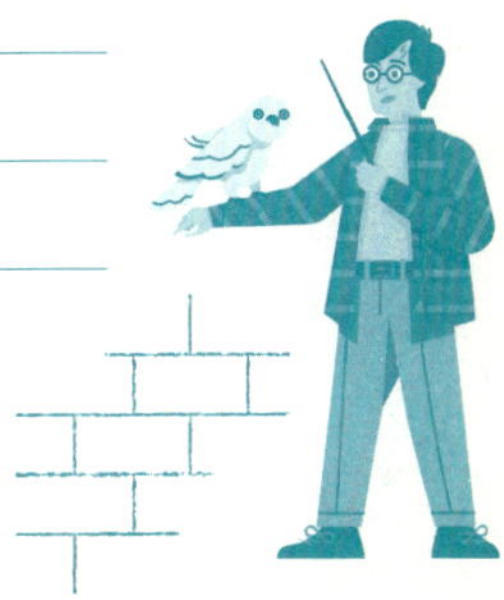

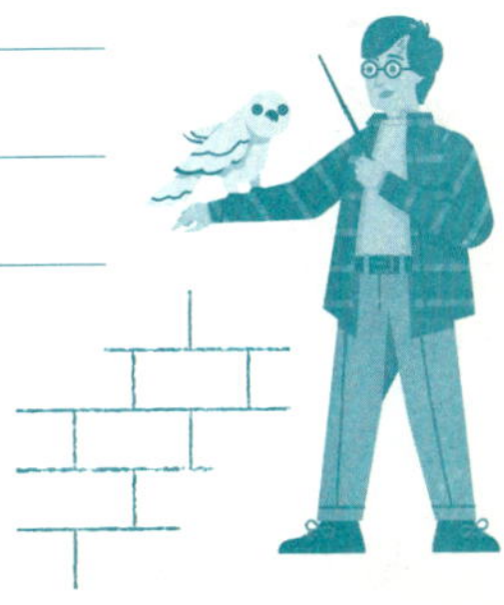

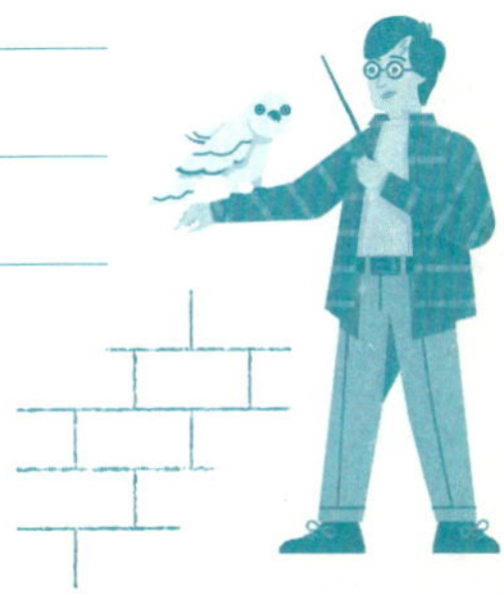

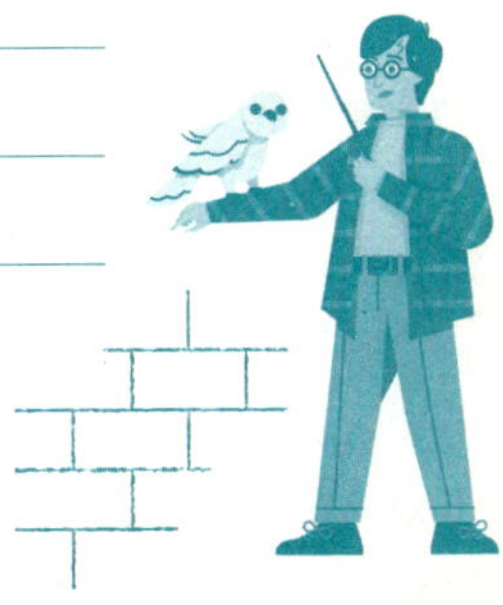

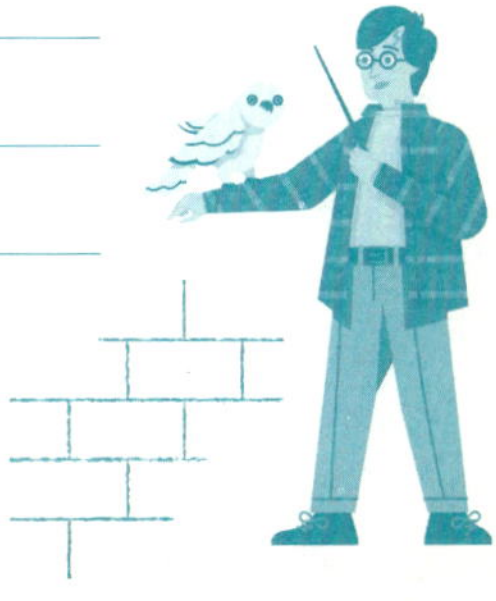

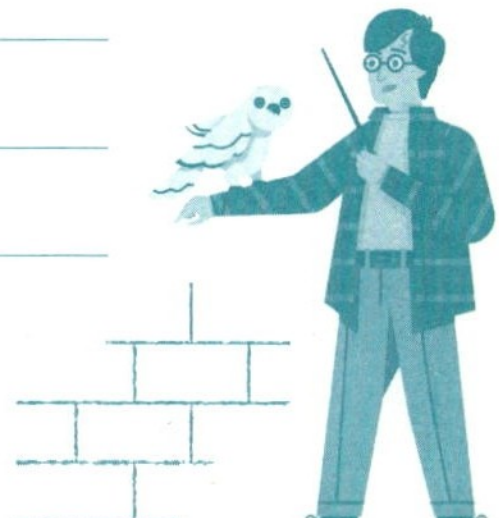

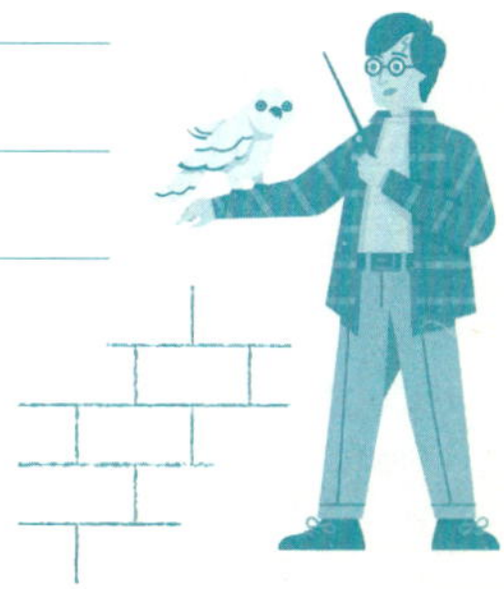

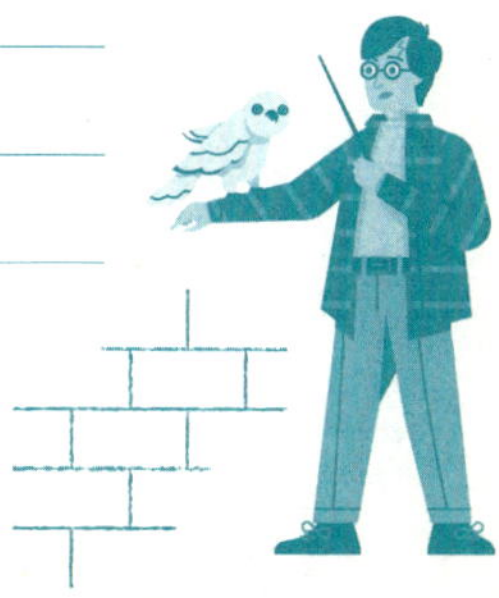

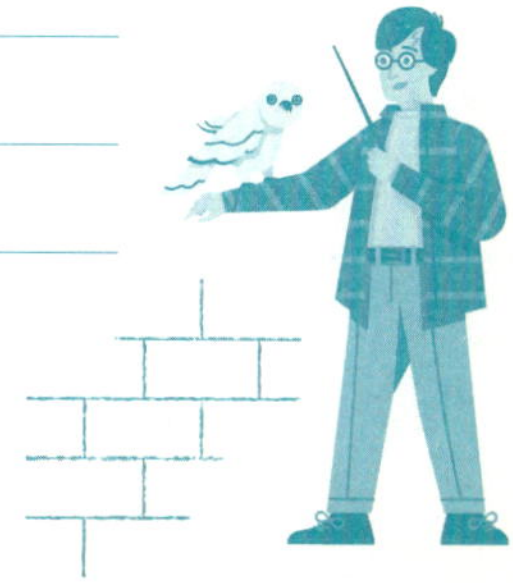

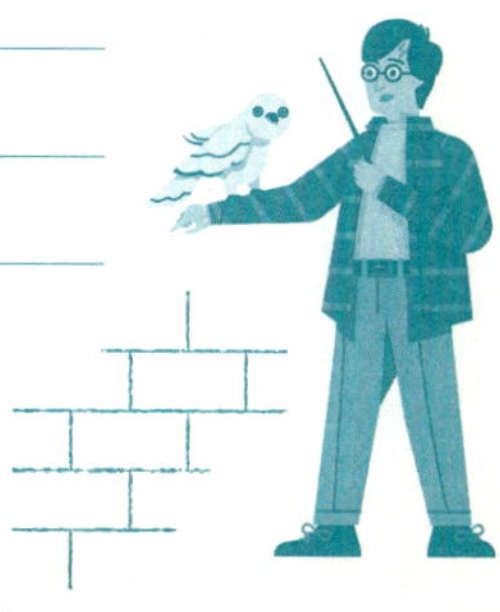

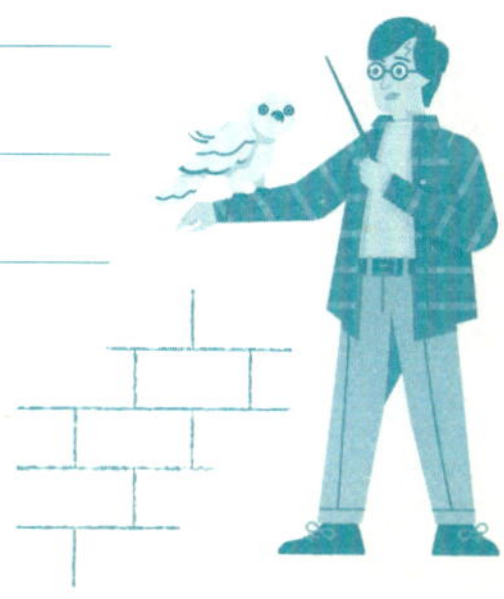

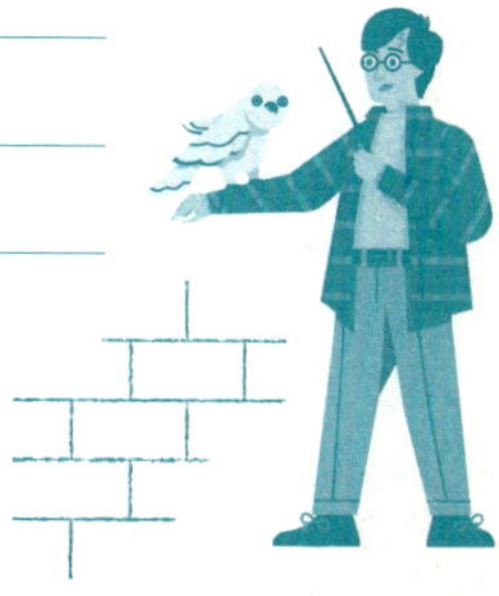

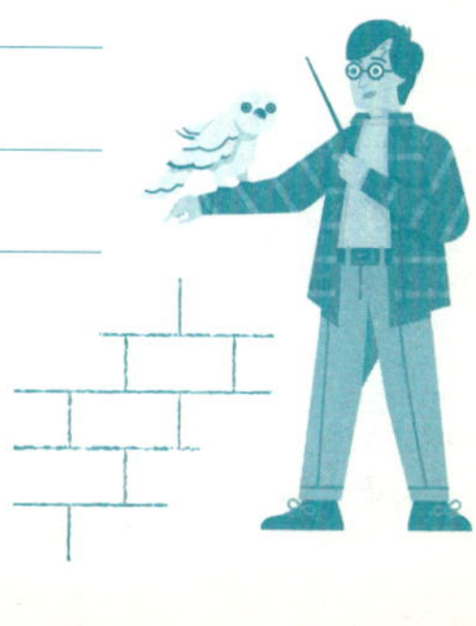

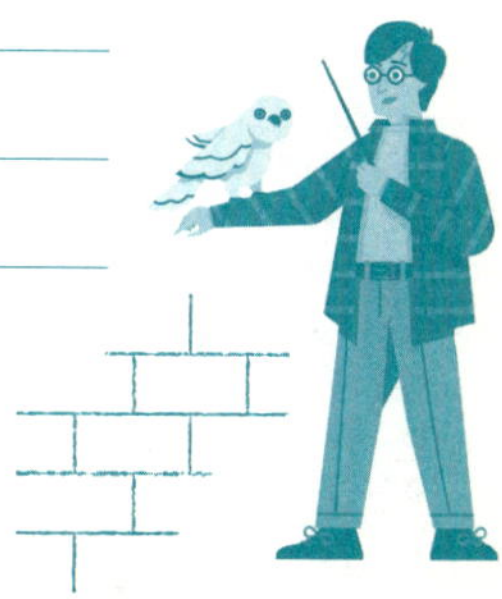

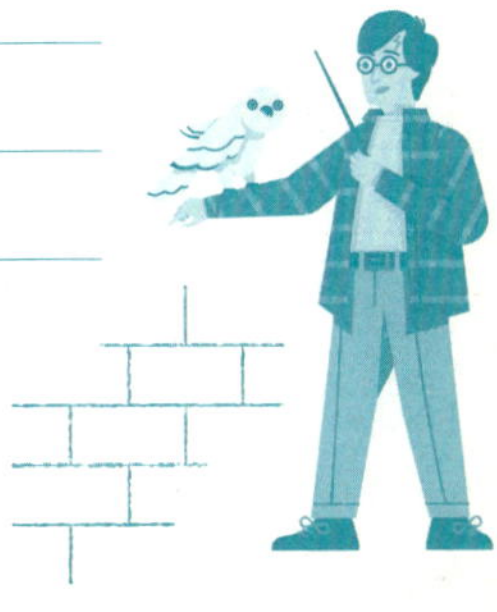

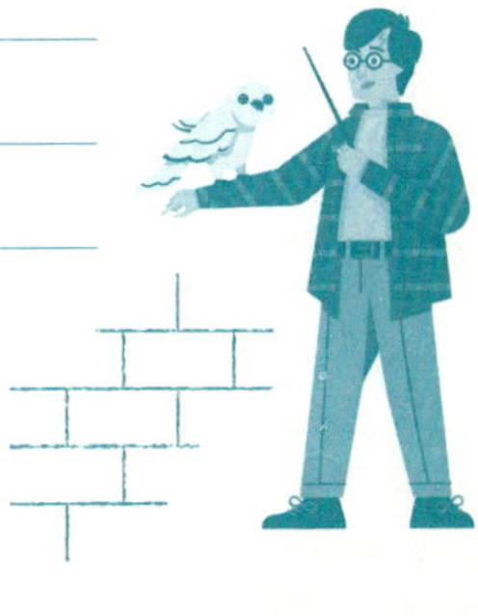

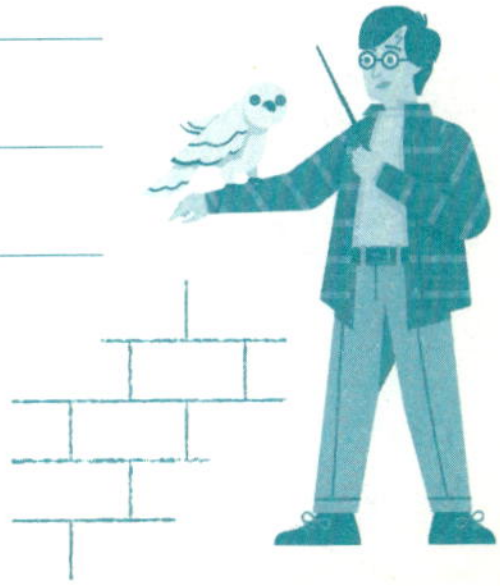

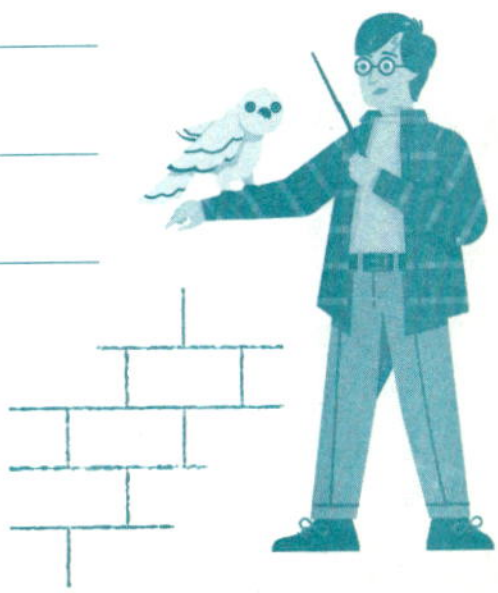

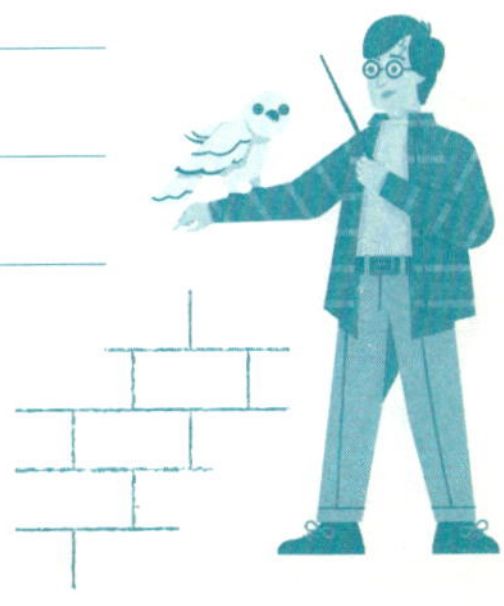

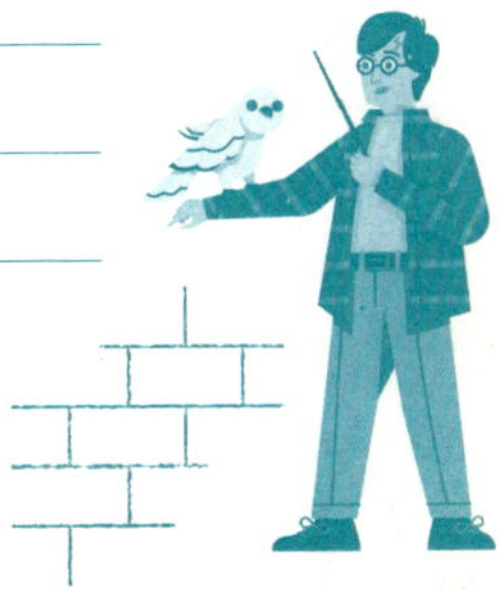

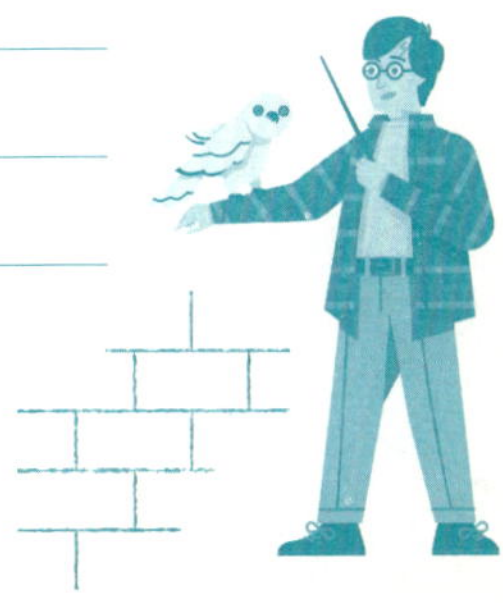

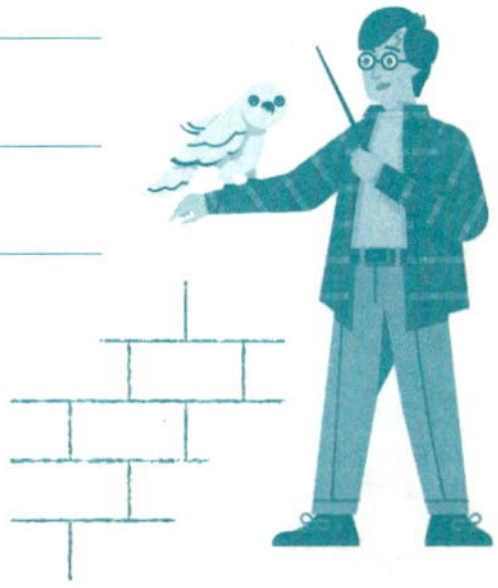

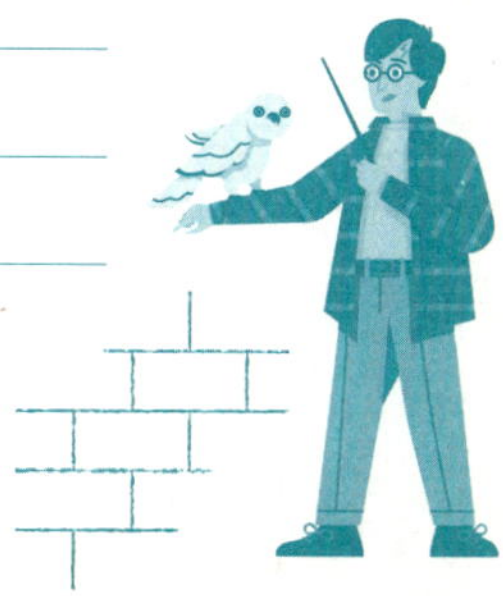

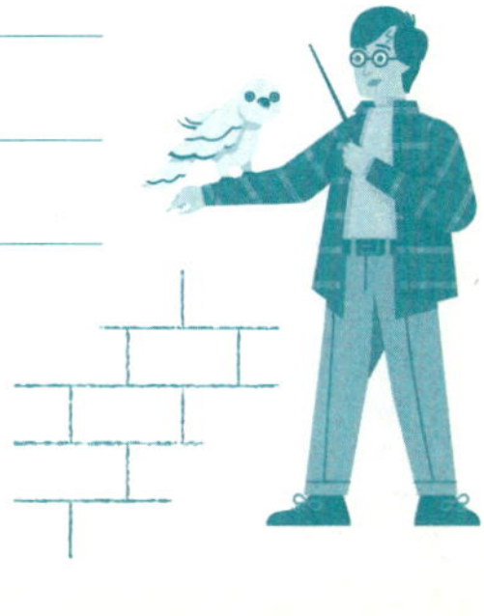

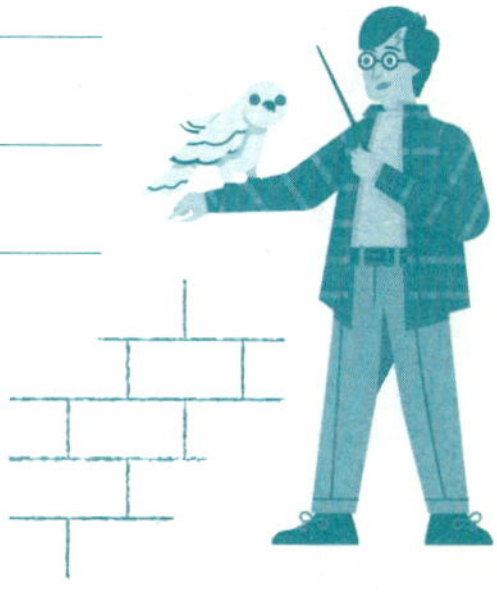

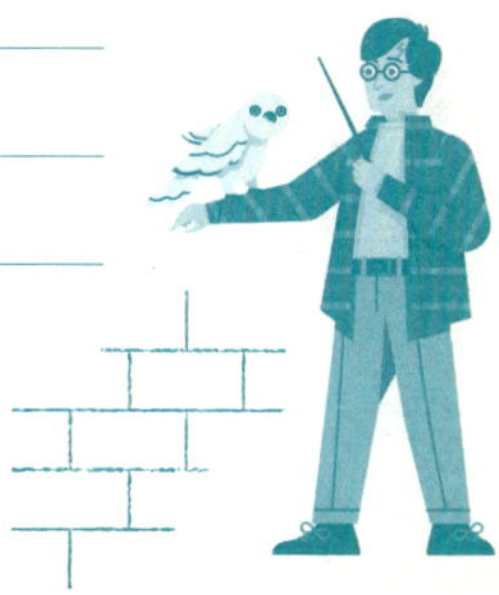

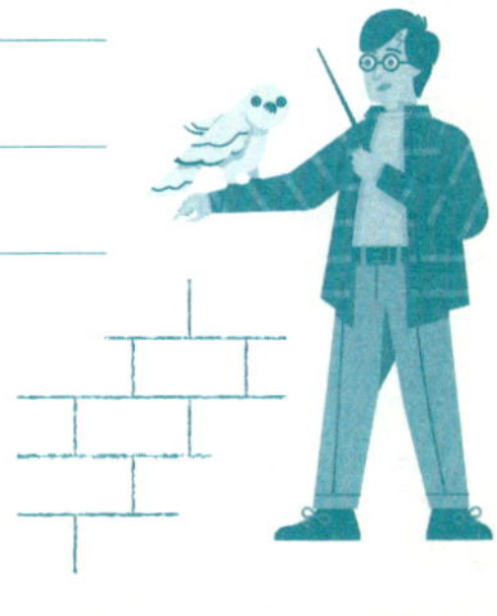

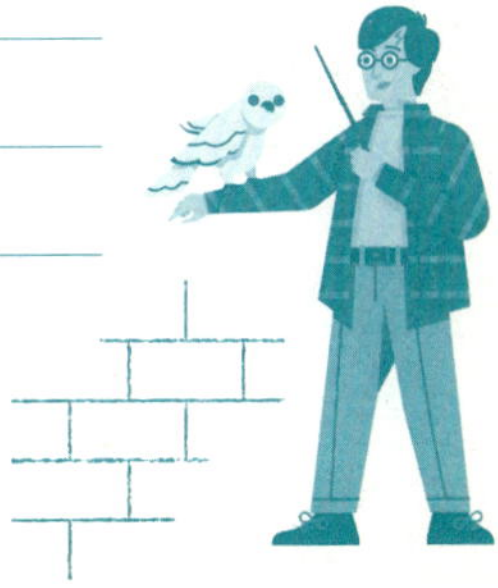

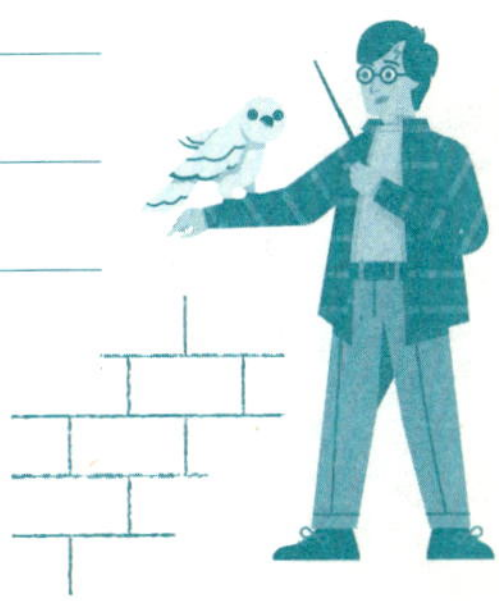

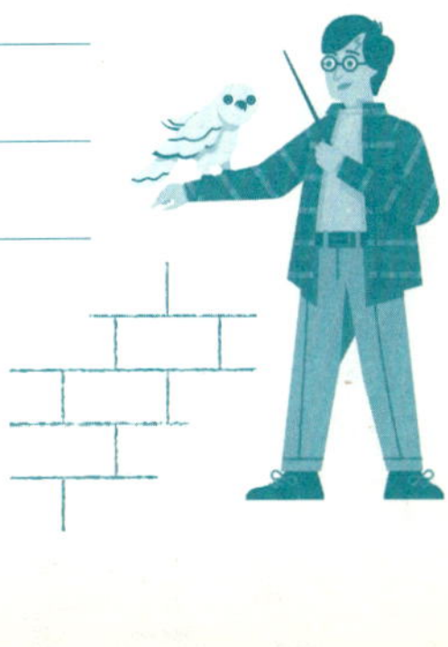

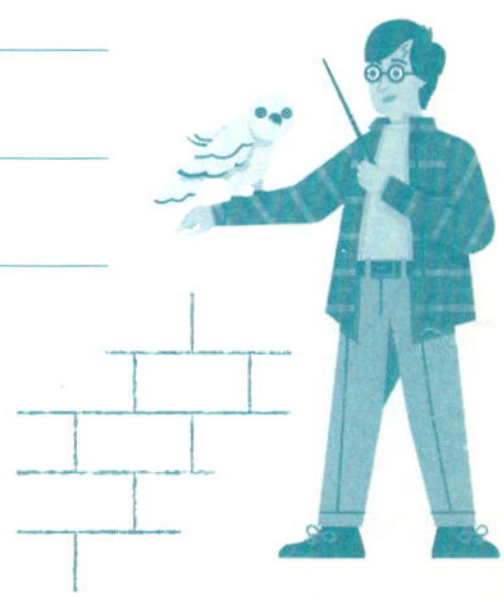

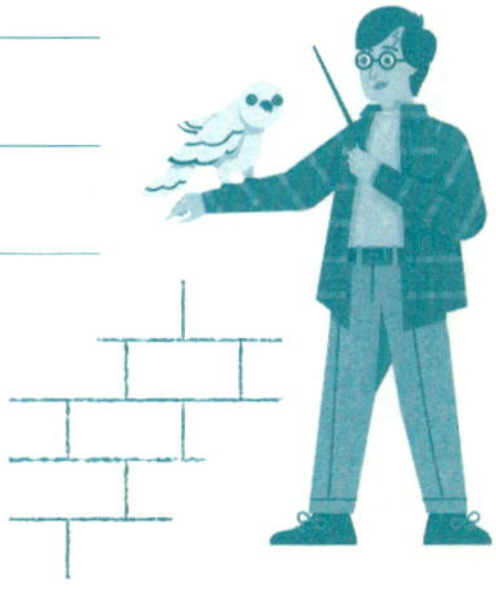

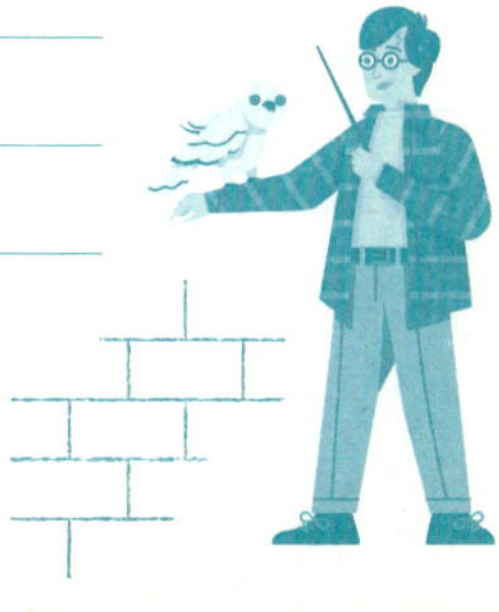

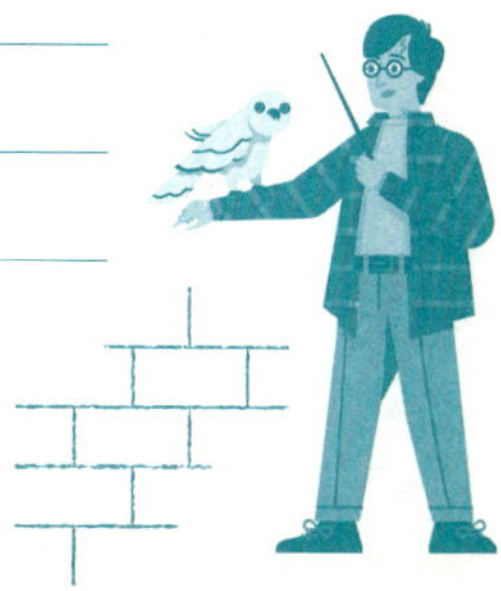

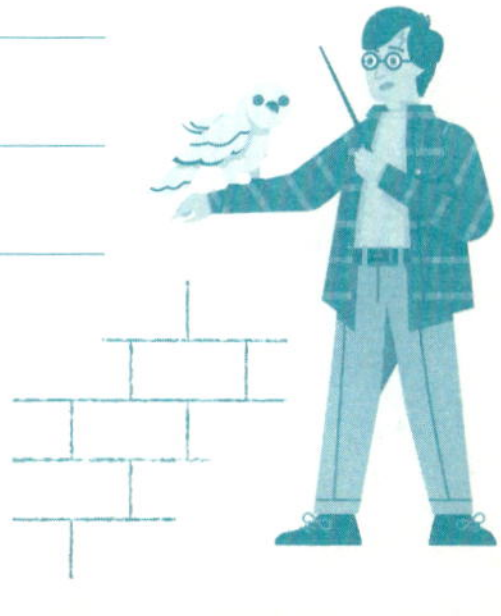

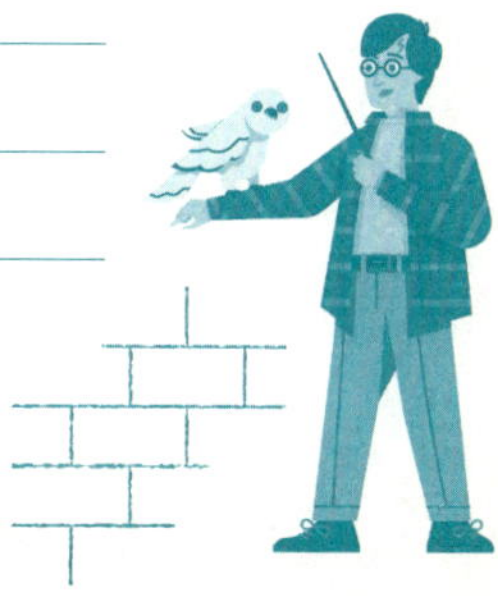

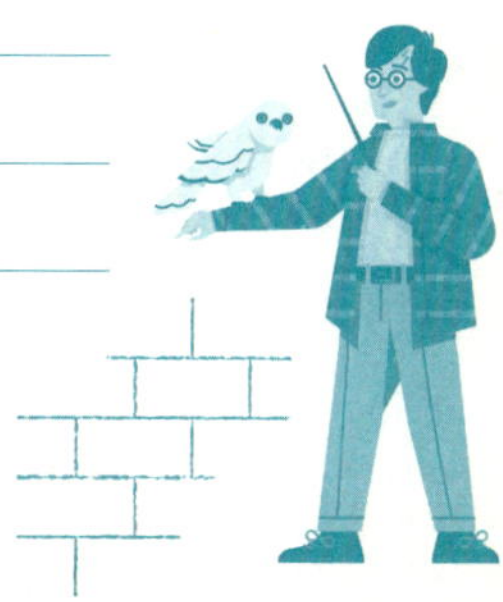

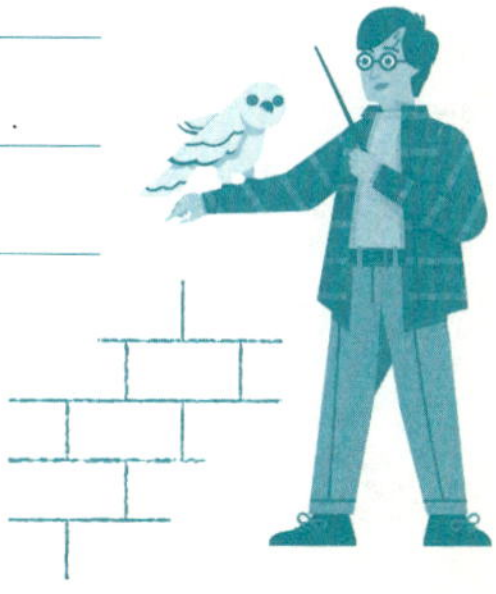

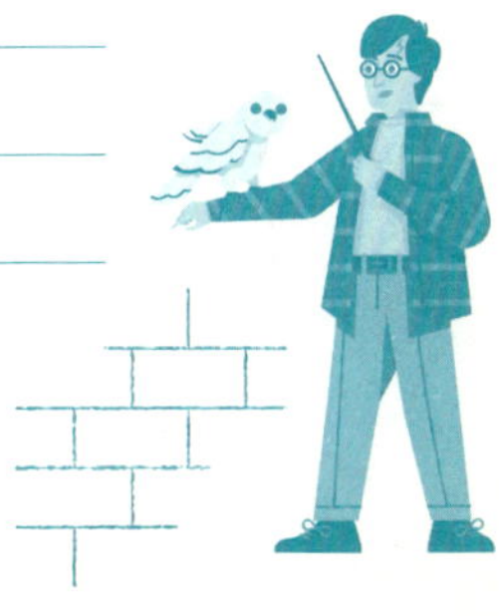

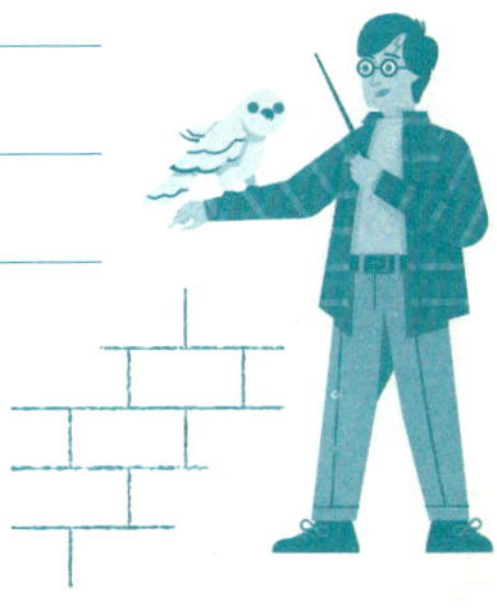

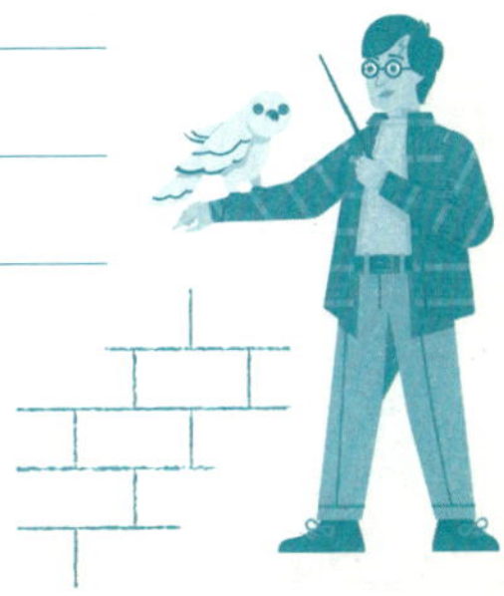

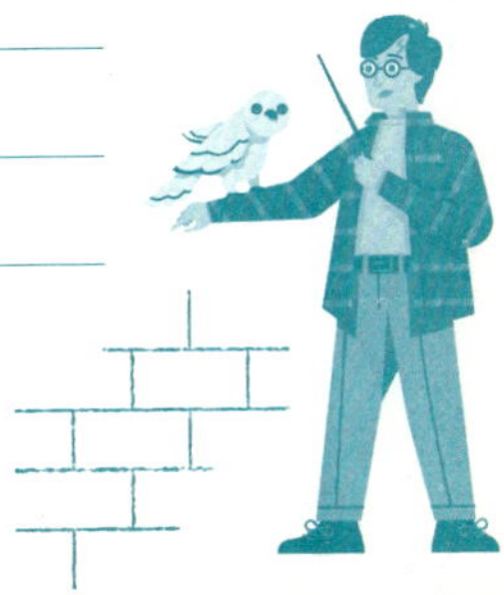

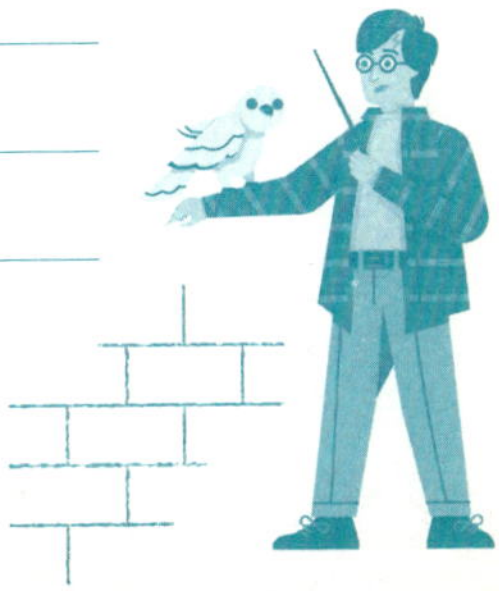

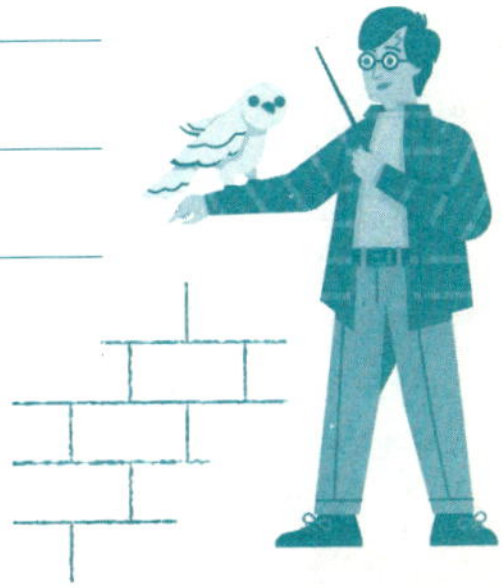

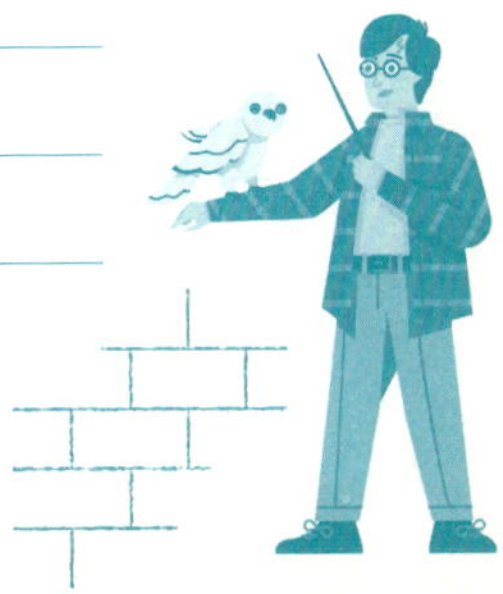

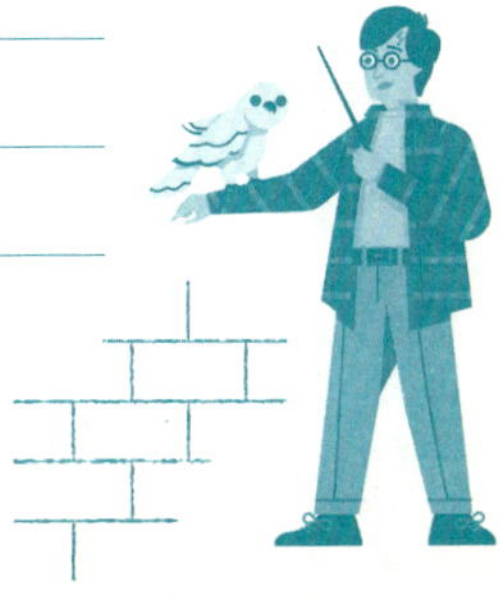

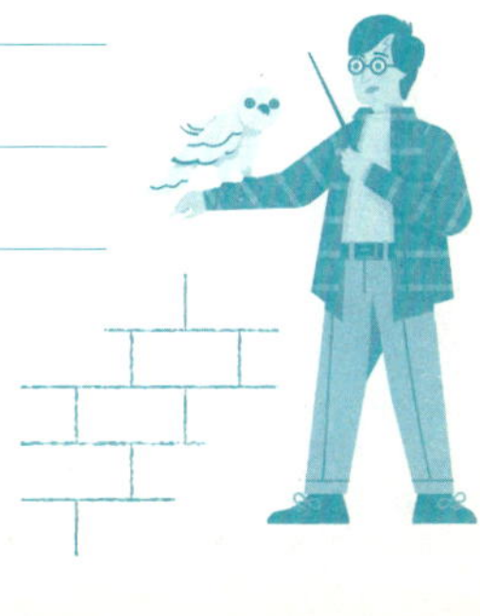

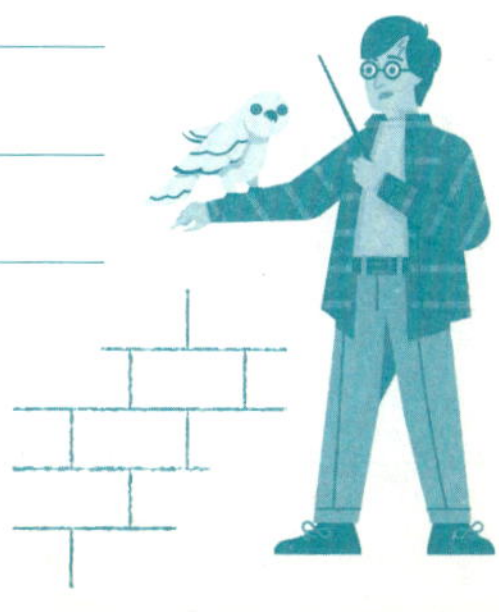

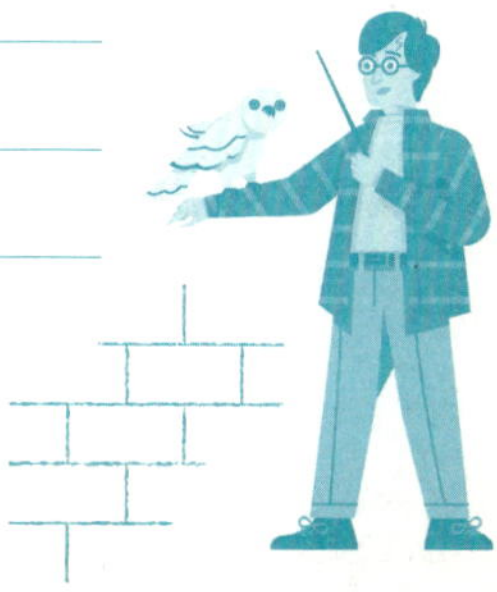

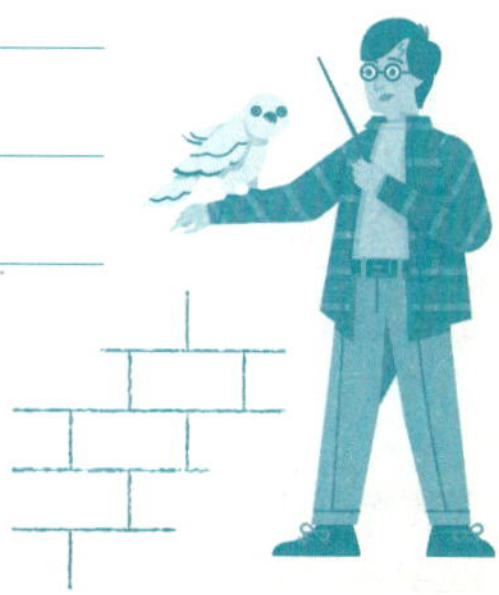

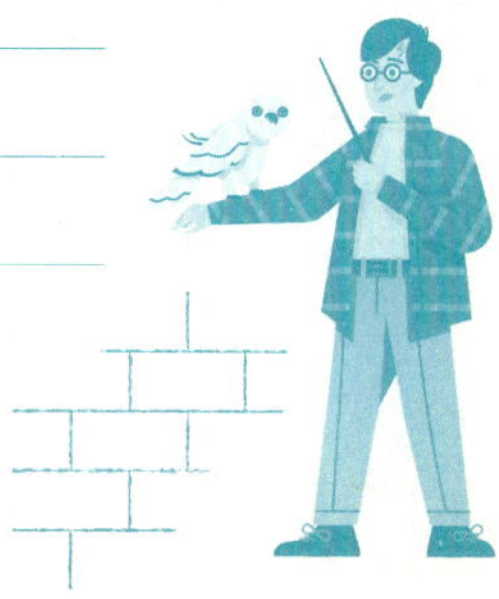

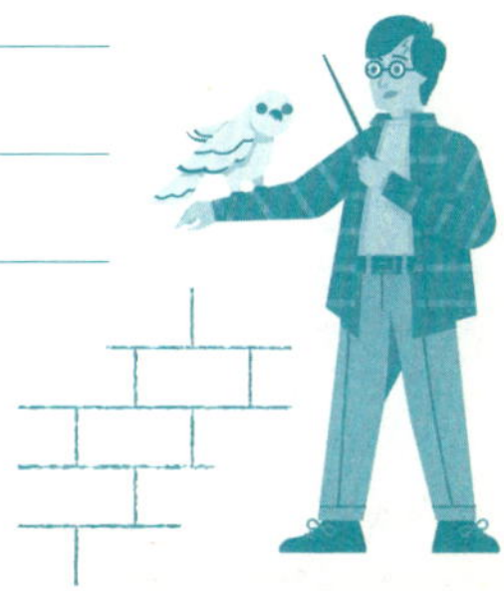

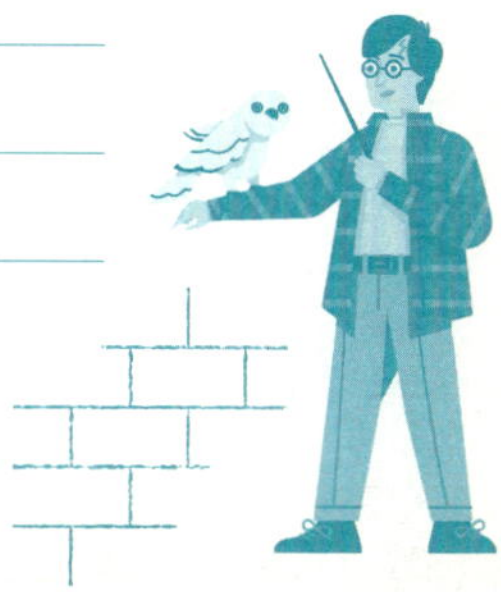

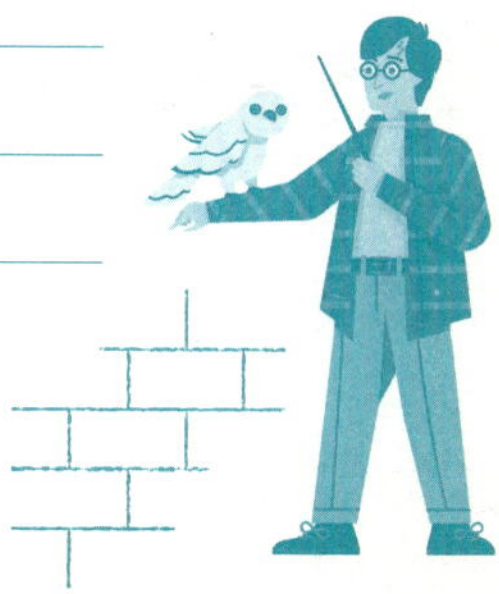

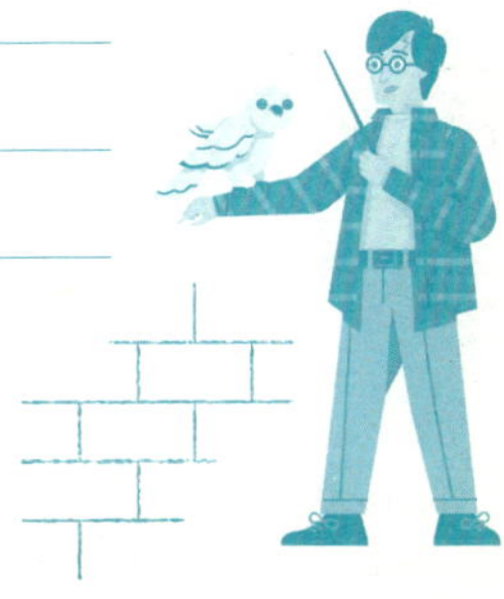

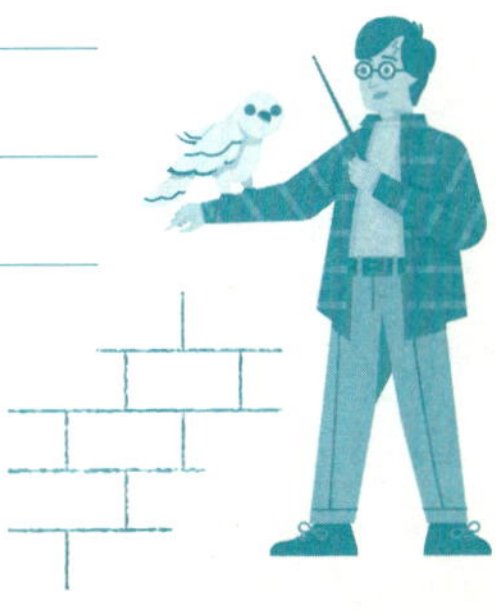

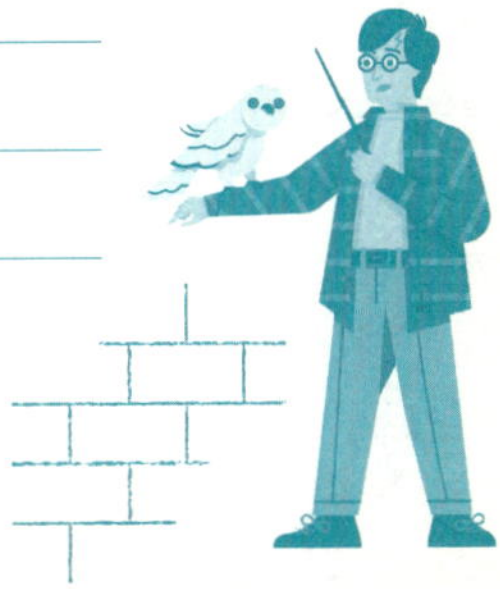

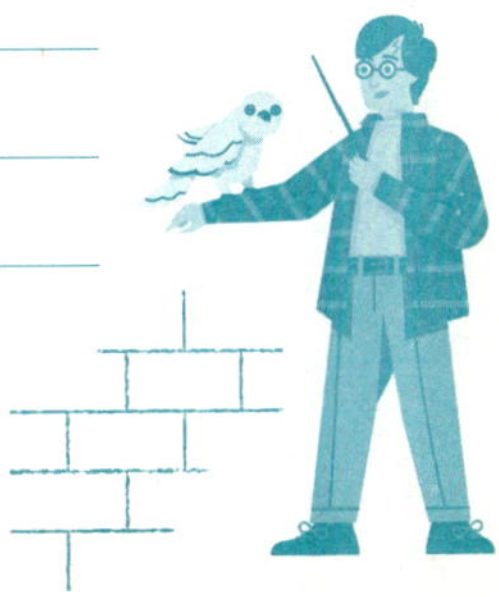

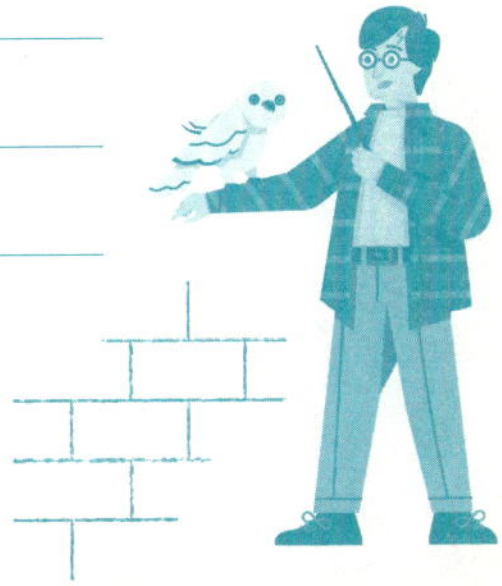

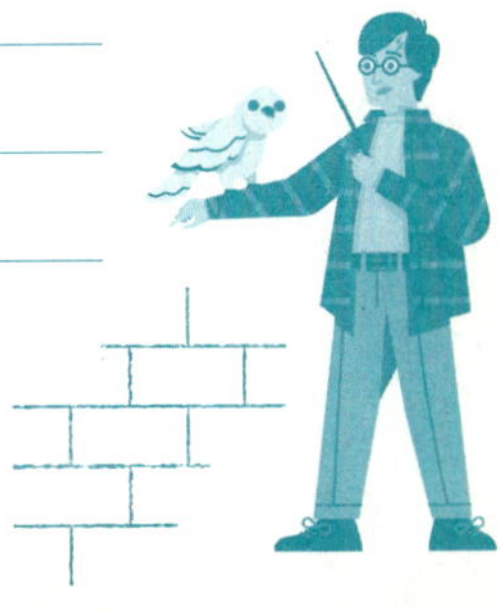

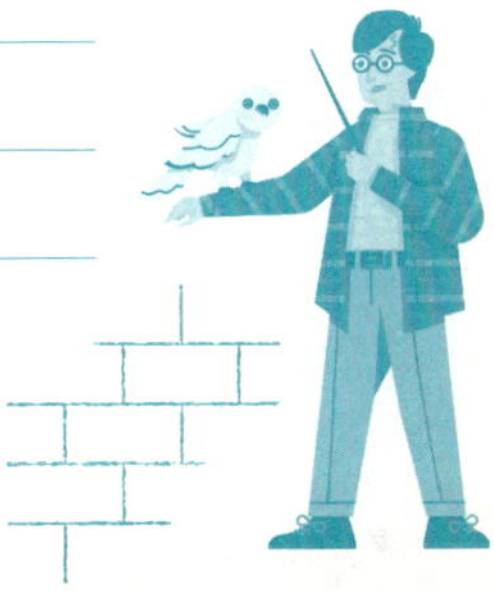

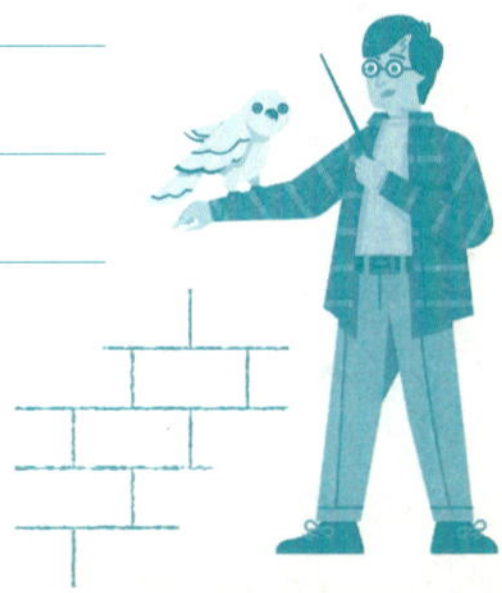

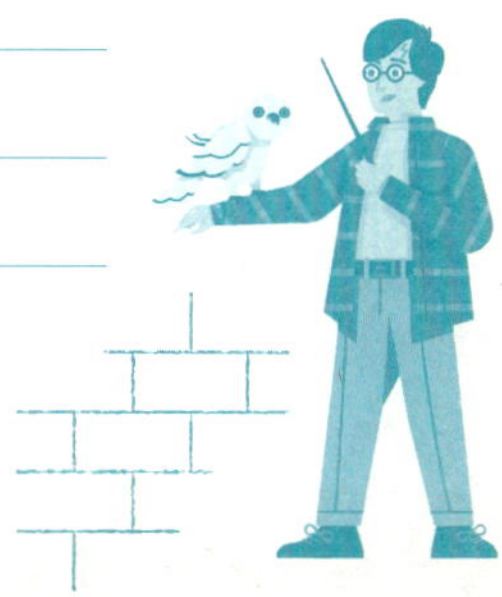

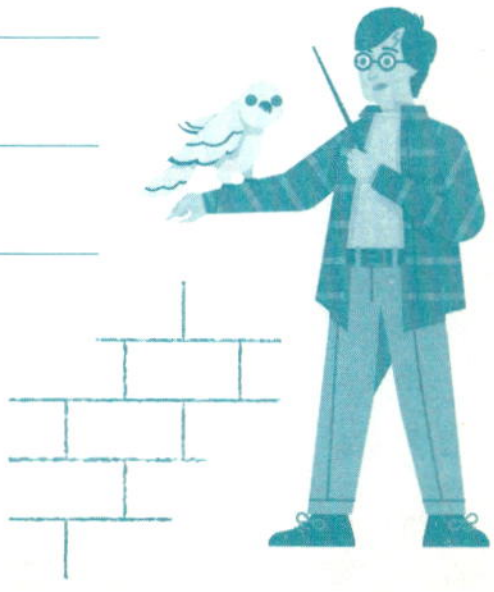

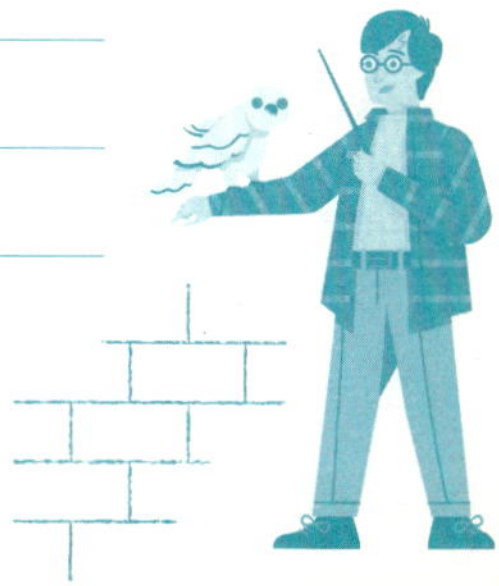

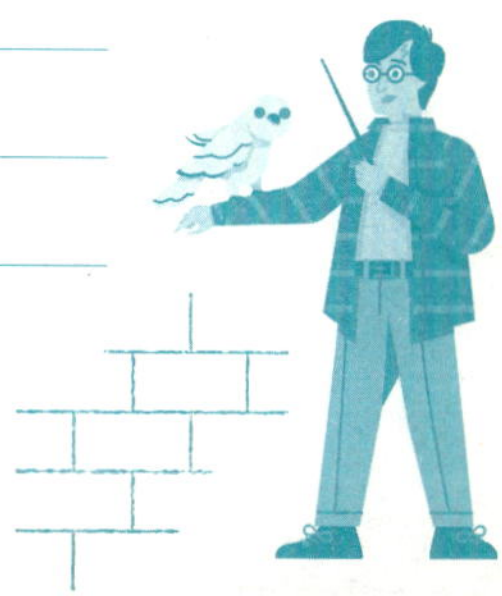

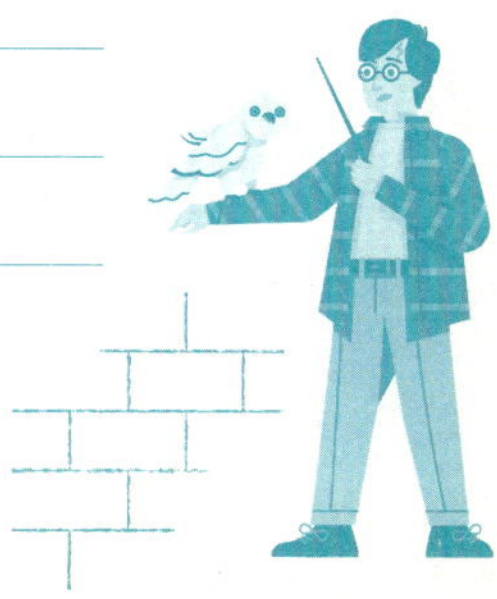

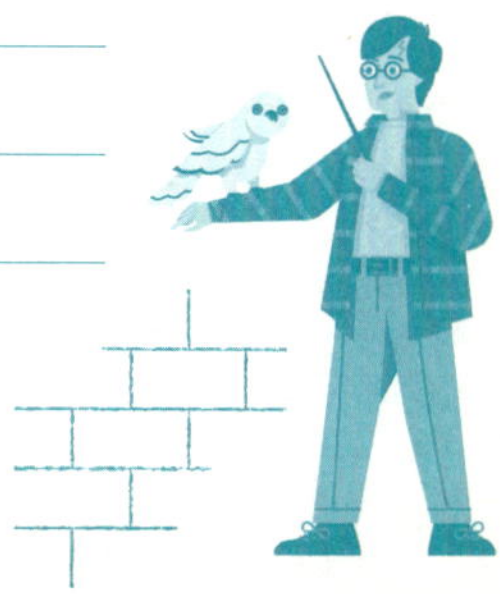

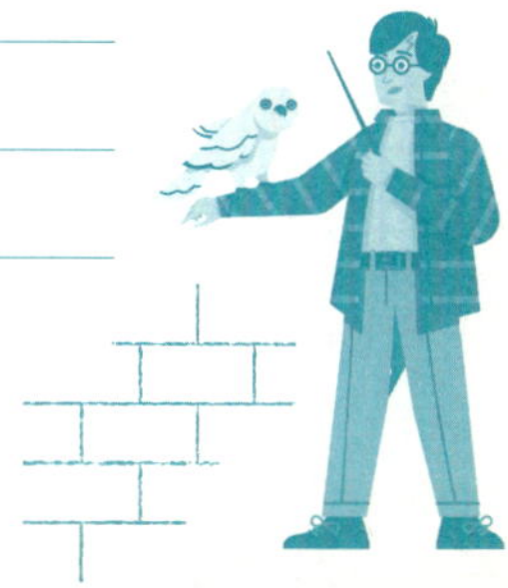

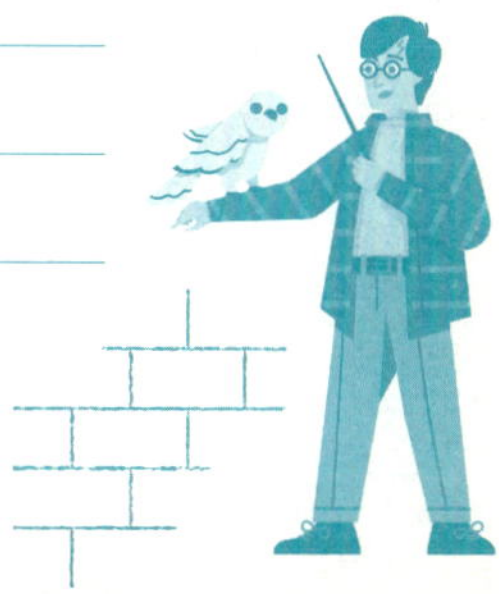

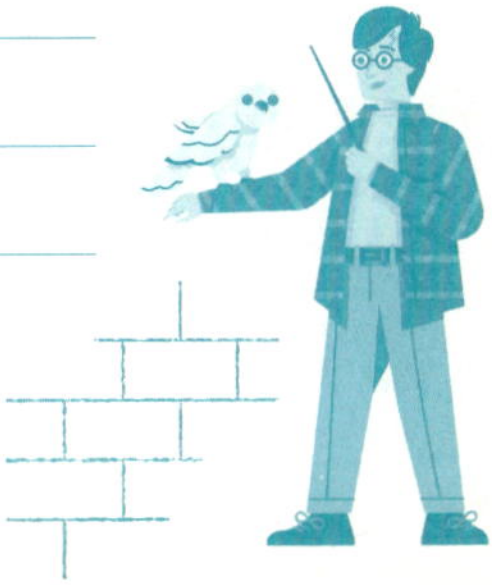

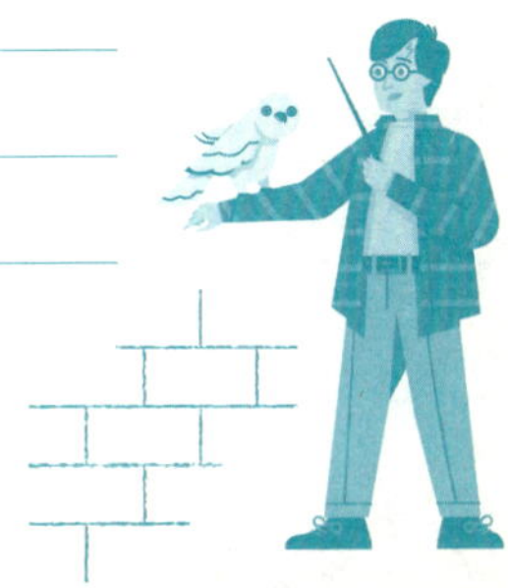

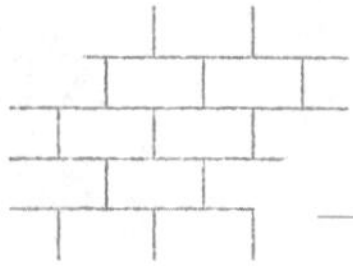

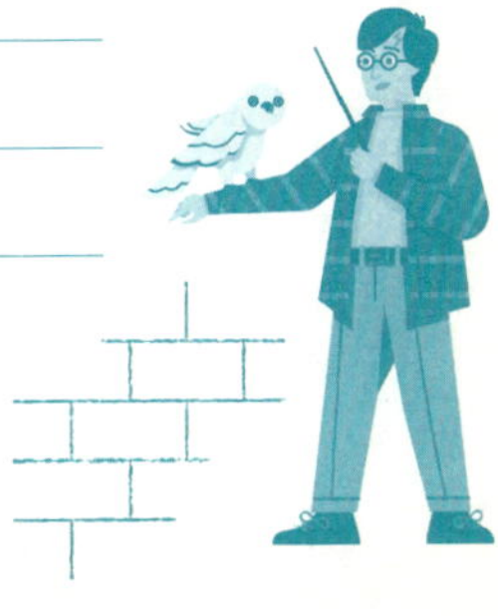

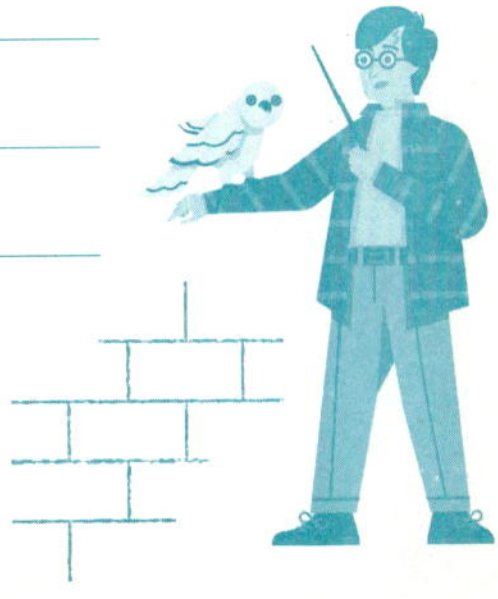

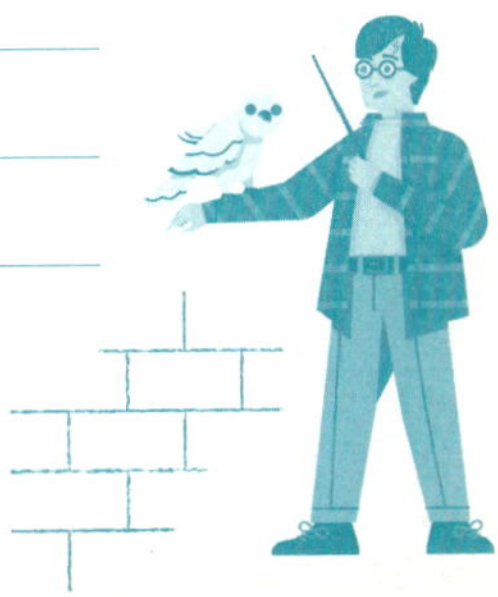

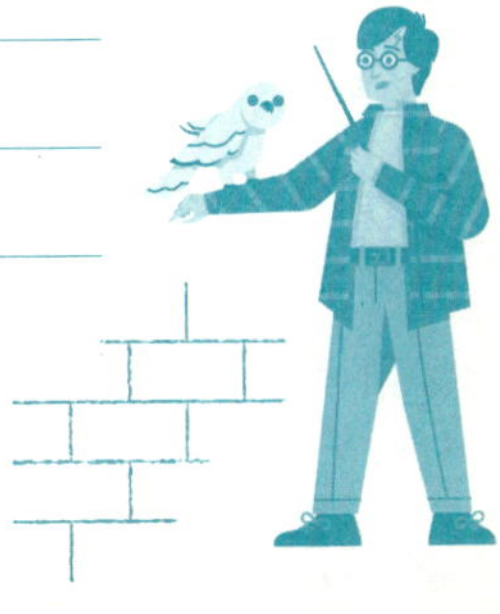

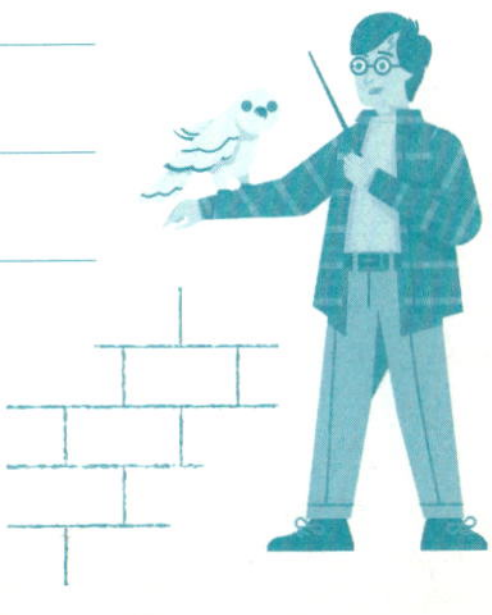

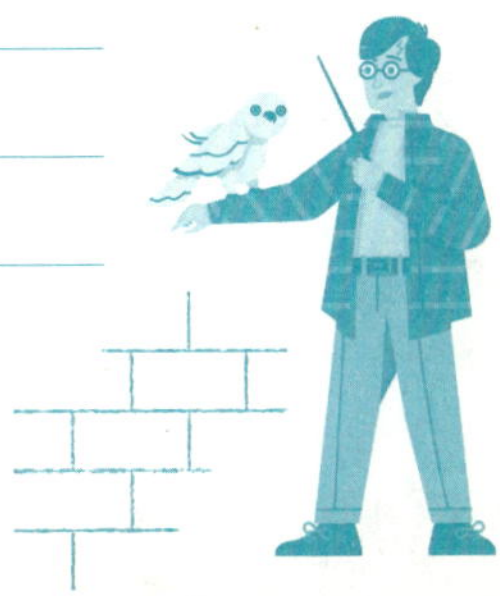

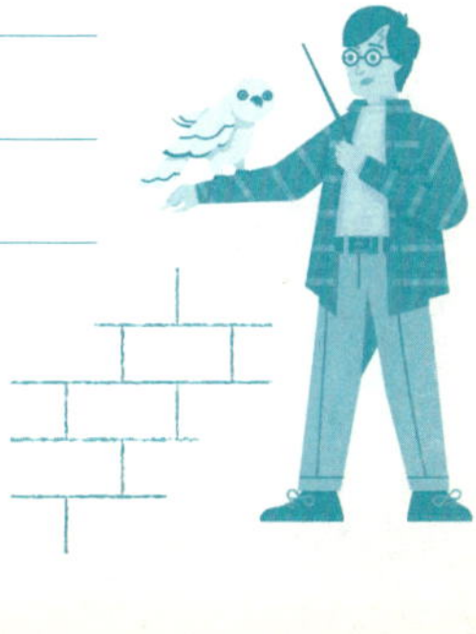

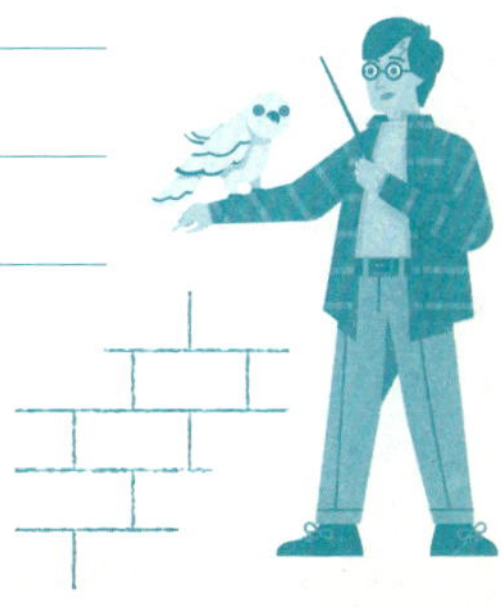

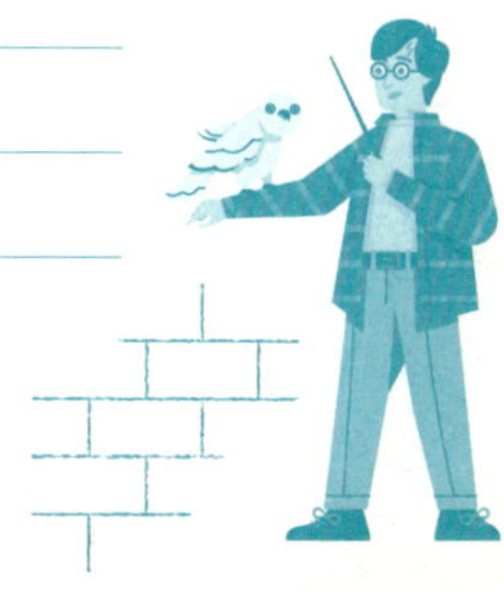

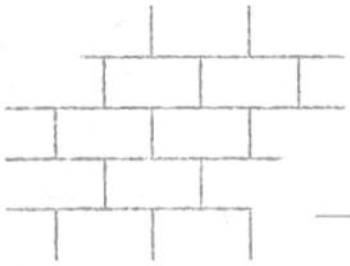

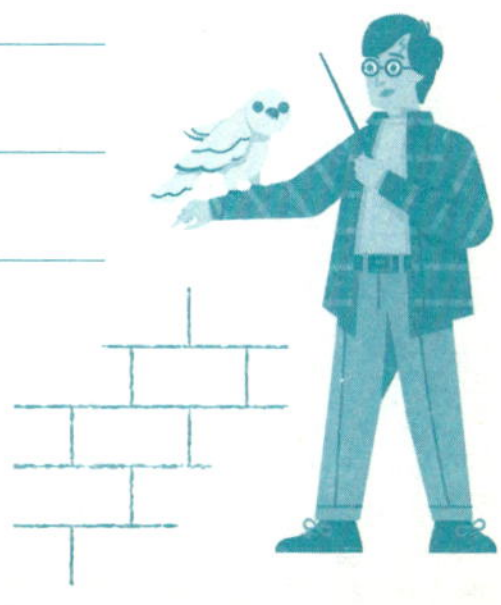

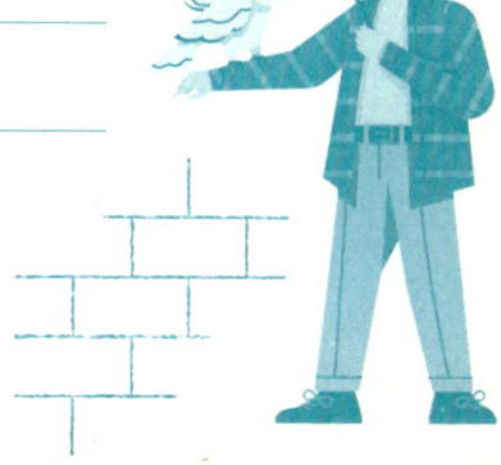

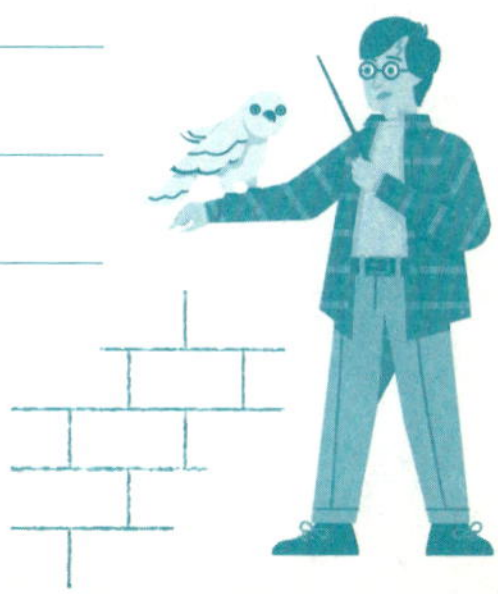

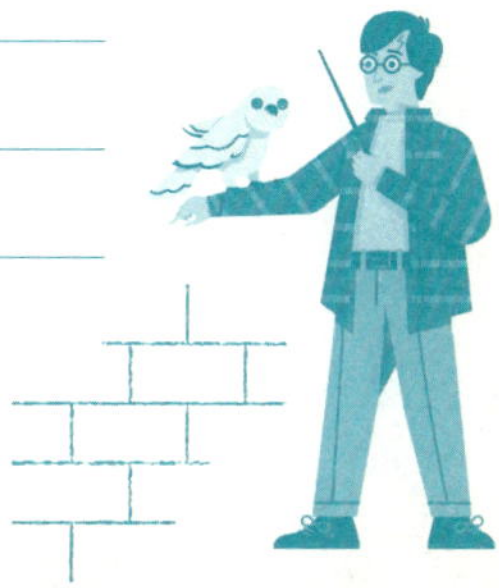

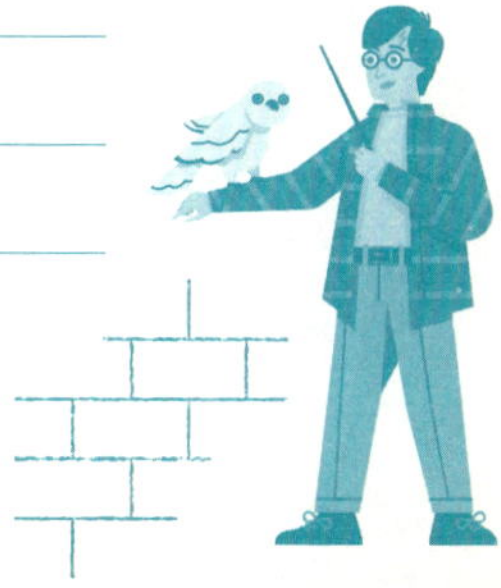

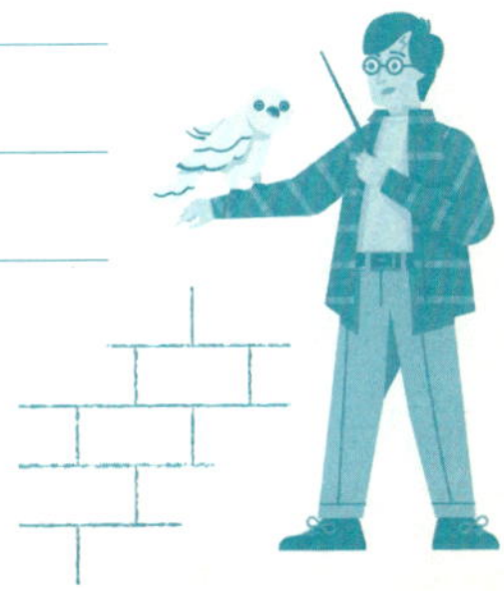

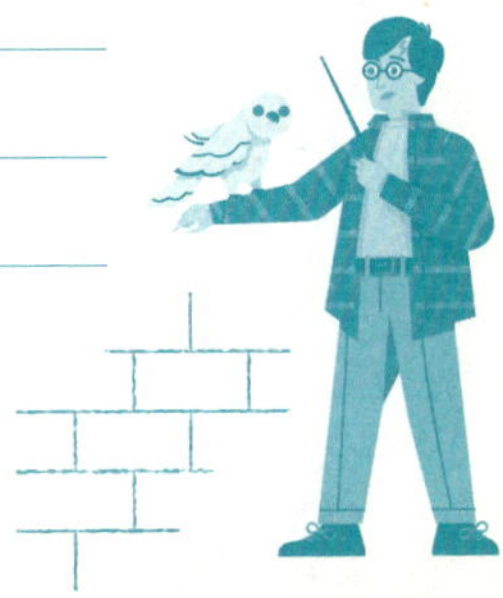

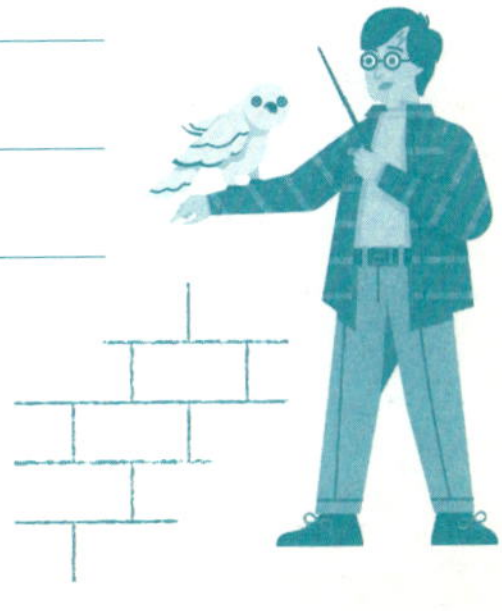

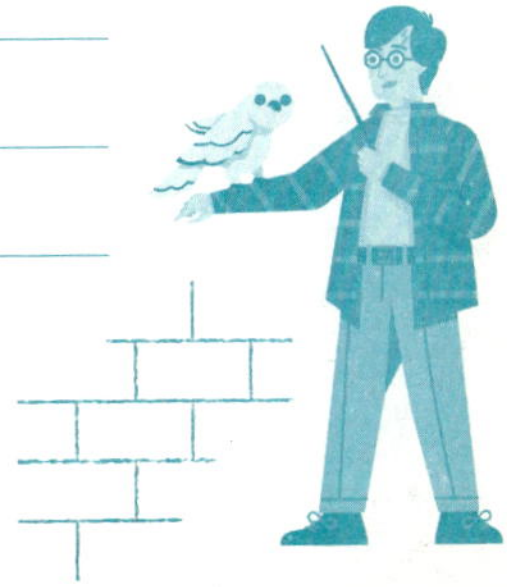

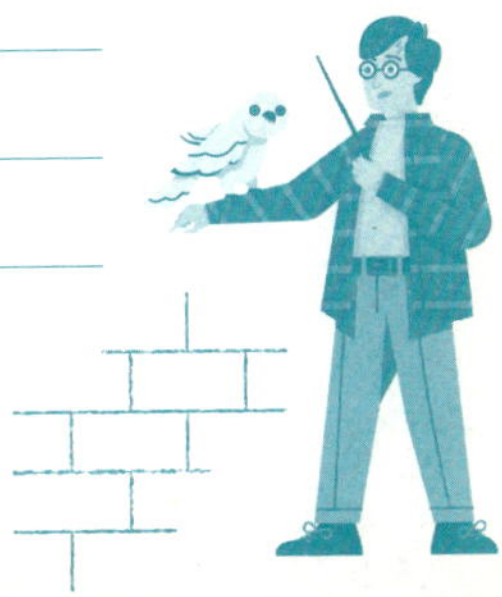

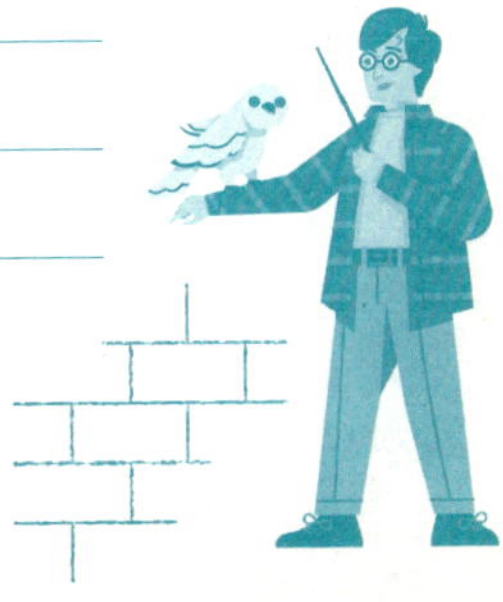

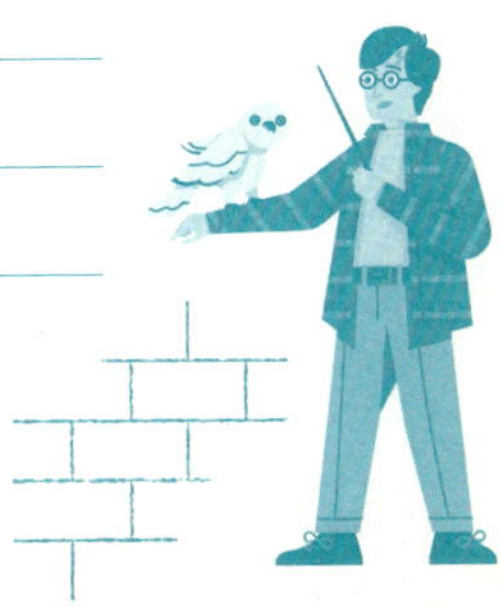

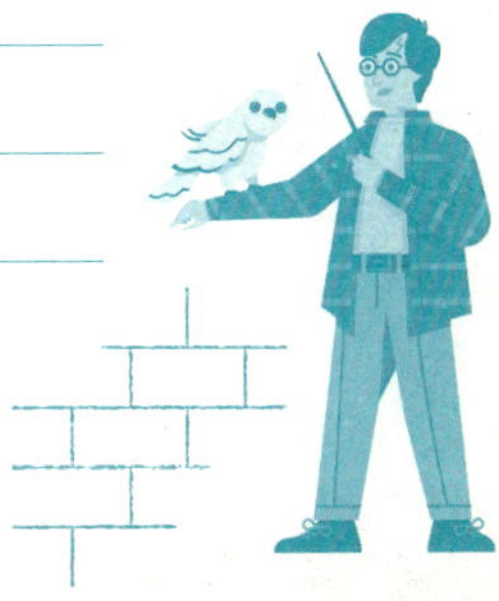

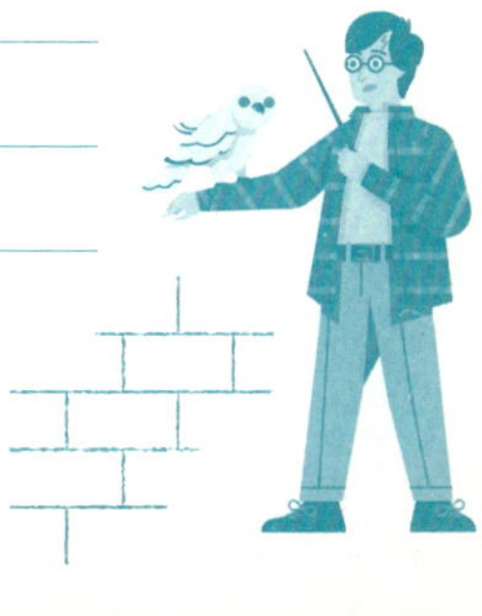

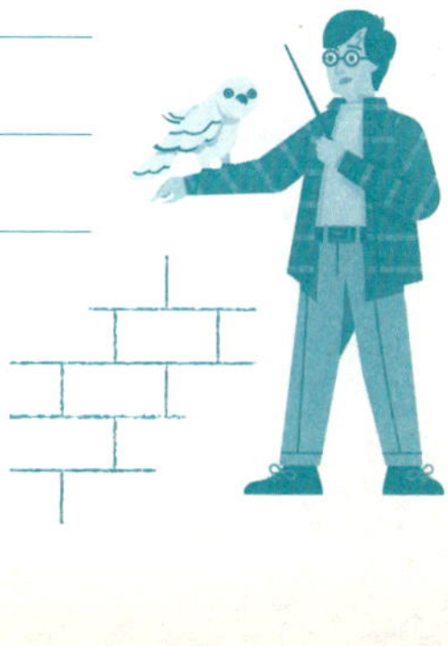

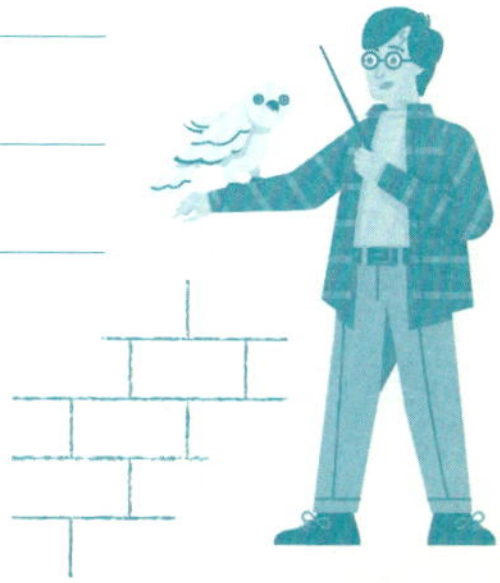

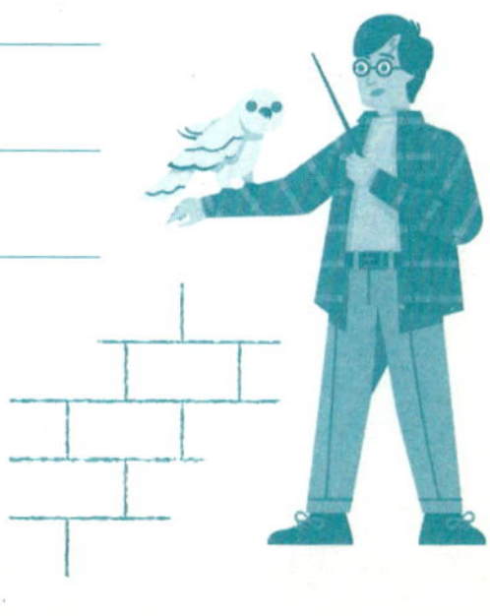

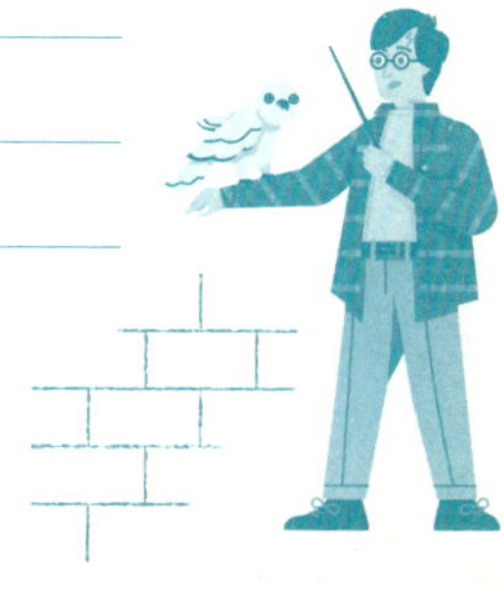

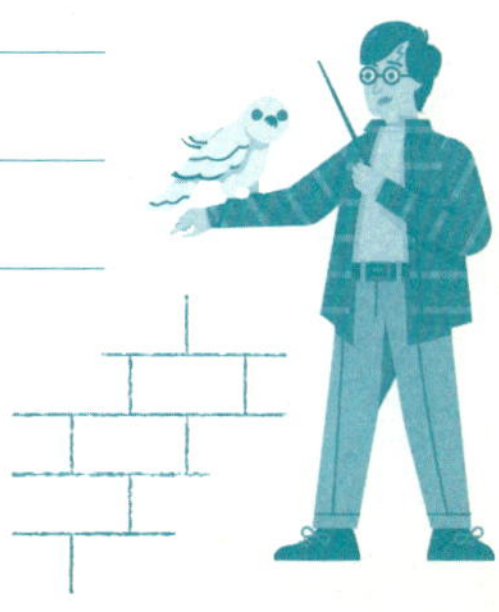

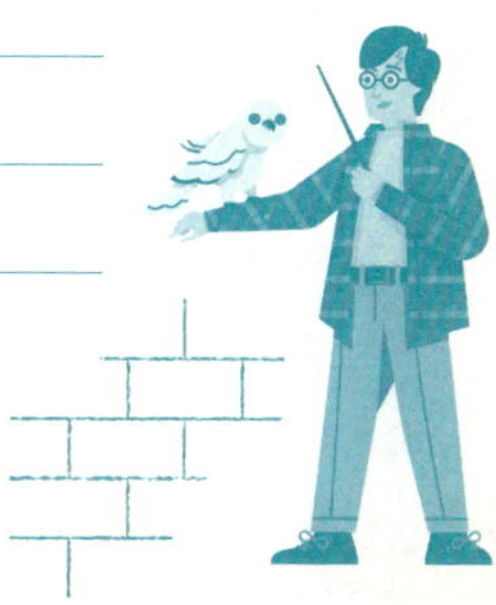

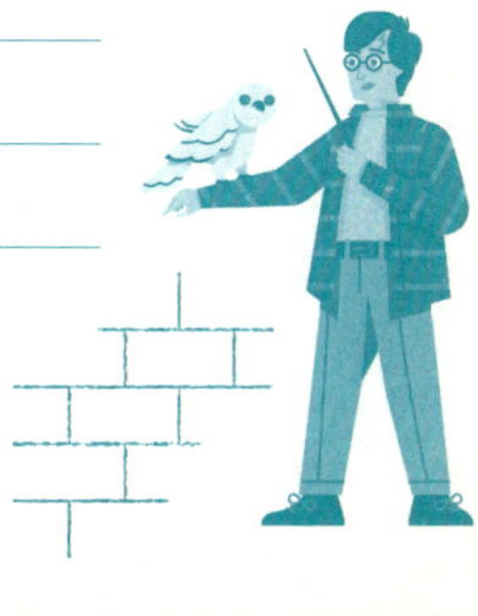

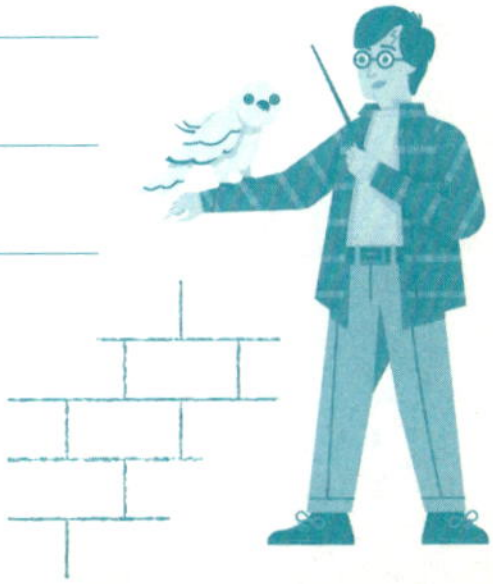

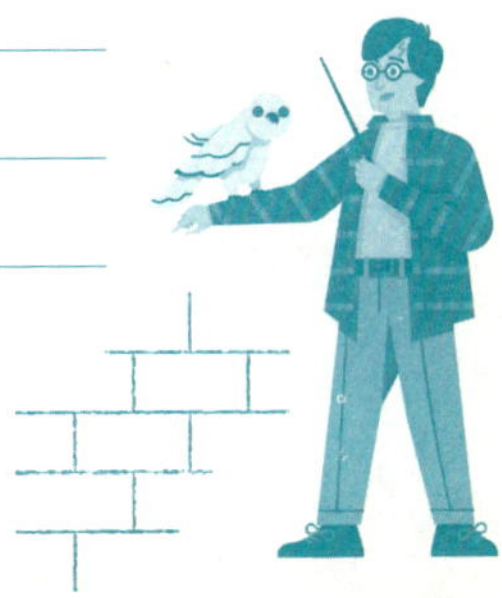

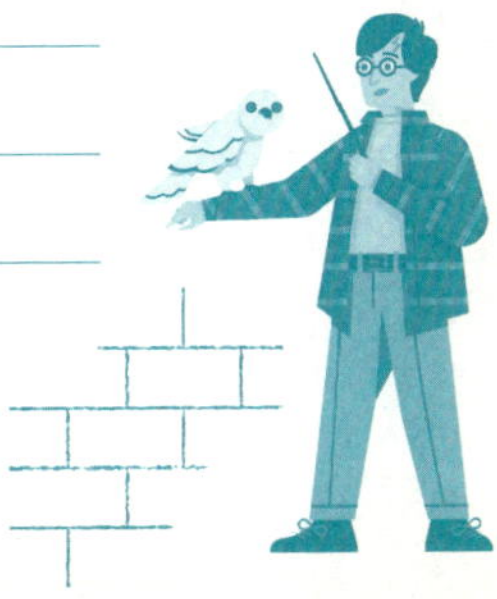

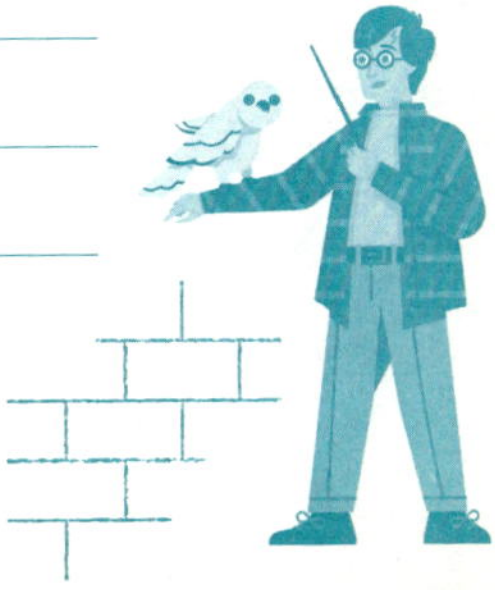

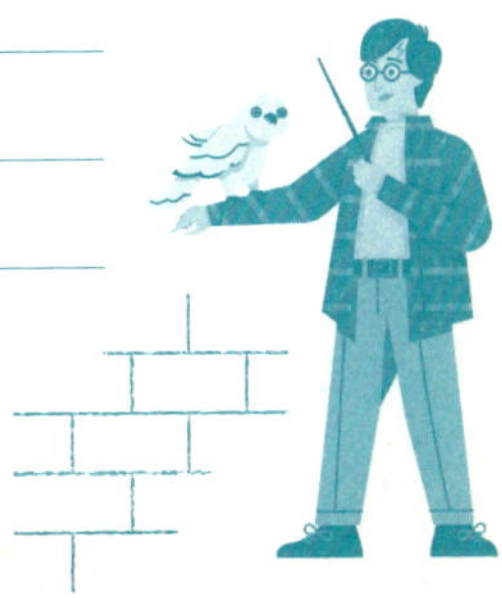

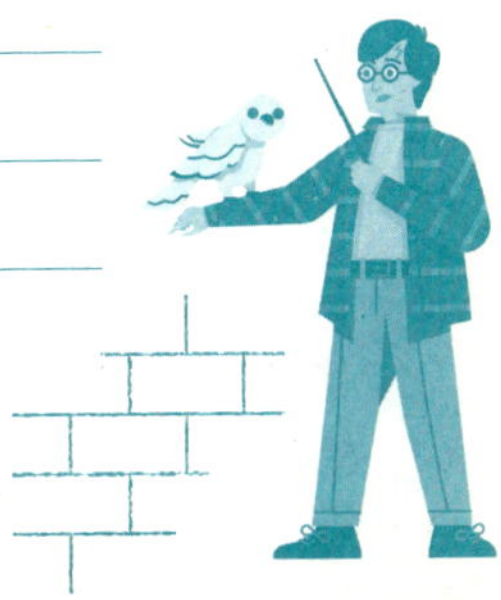

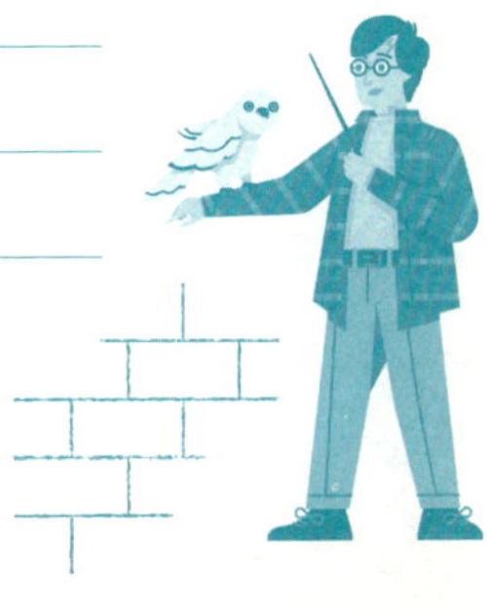

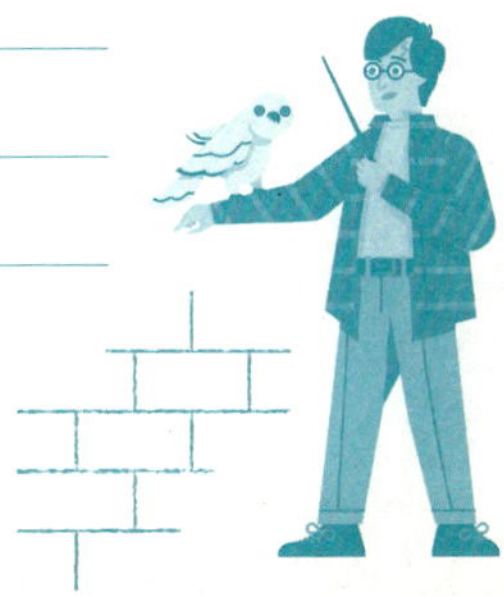

Harry Potter™

Illustrations by Studio Muti.

INSIGHTS
an imprint of
INSIGHT EDITIONS
www.insighteditions.com

MANUFACTURED IN CHINA

10 9 8 7 6 5 4 3

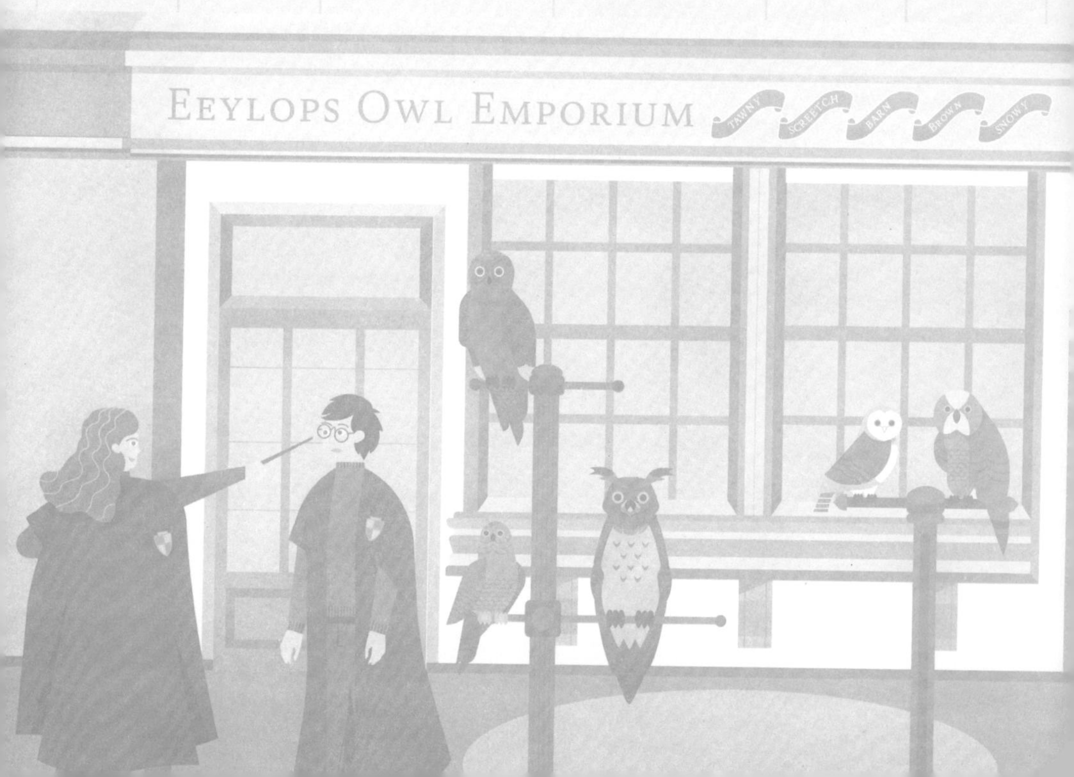

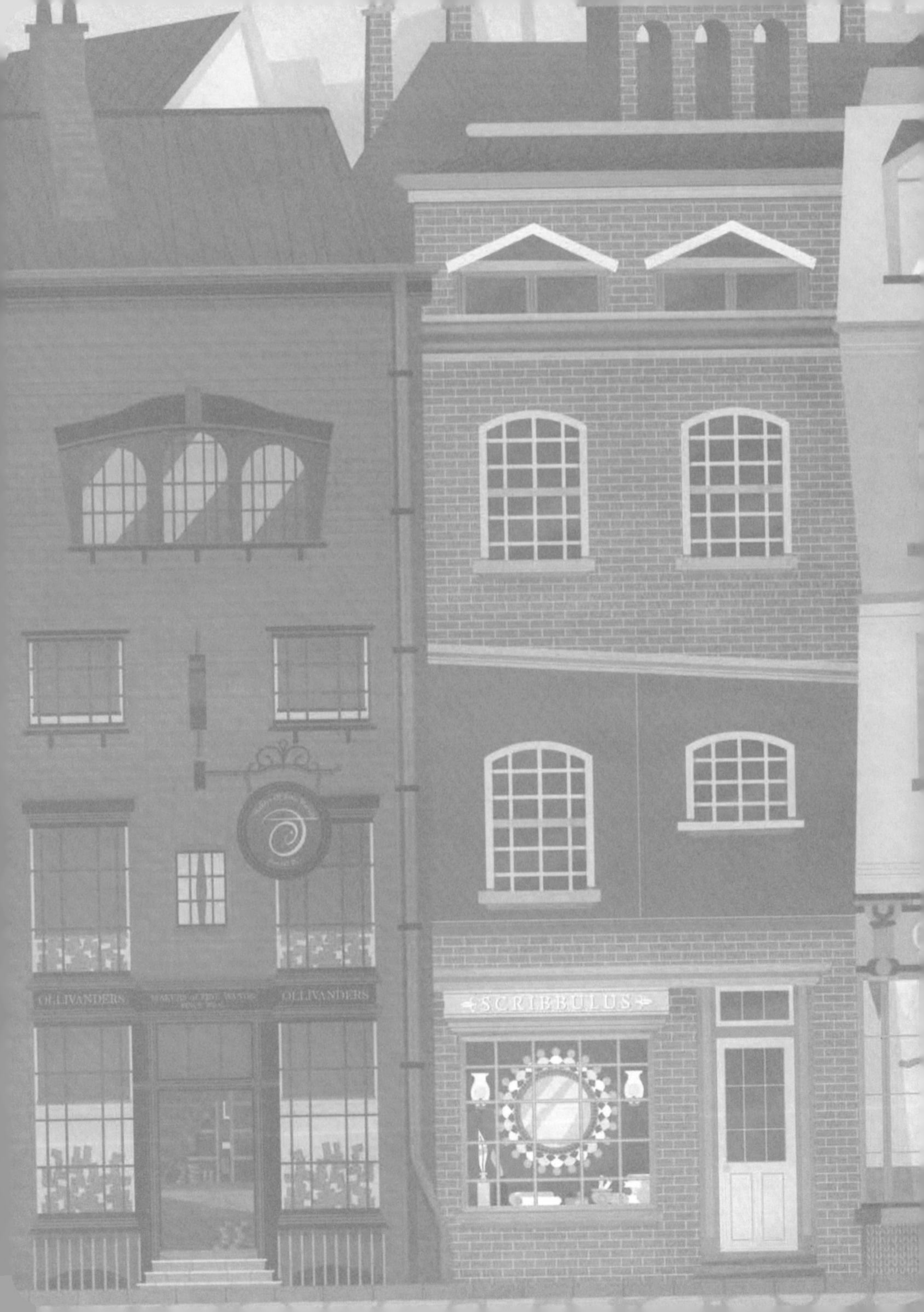
OLLIVANDERS
OLLIVANDERS
SCRIBBULUS